Praise for *The Fort*

"Underground tunnels, war stories, thieves, and hidden gold...what's not to like? Any lover of history and an old fashion, wholesome adventure will enjoy THE FORT."

Marc Cameron, author of the best-selling Jericho Quinn thriller series, and most recently "Power and Empire", the latest Jack Ryan novel in the popular Tom Clancy series.

Other Books By Eldon DeKay

The Closet

The Mine

The Quake

The Cabin

The Fort

By

Eldon DeKay

<u>DEDICATION</u>

This book is dedicated to my beautiful and infinitely
supportive wife, whose

accompaniment on all of the adventures that inspired
this book, and most

of the rest of my life, has been continual and appreciated

Prologue

The War was beyond brutal. The battle had been going on for months, waxing and waning with the German assaults. The German command planned for Verdun to be the downfall of the French army. They amassed incomprehensible quantities of artillery and munitions before the battle began, digging in to the north of the city. On a well-developed railway system they deployed gigantic guns which could be moved around the battlefield to bombard the defending French to their south. The French were positioned around a ring of forts and trenches built in the late 1800s. The French had also built a railway network for supply and attack and had stockpiled their own artillery and ammunition.

The battle had started on February 21, 1916 as the Germans unleashed 1,000,000 shells from 808 guns in the first 10 hours. The sound was continuous as one explosion could not be distinguished from the next. The Germans advanced, but the French held the high ground. Over the next 300 days the opponents traded positions repeatedly in nearly unending artillery fire. The 750,000 casualties during this time were split nearly evenly between the two sides. In the end, the Germans withdrew to the lines they had held before the battle began.

In order to keep their troops fresh, the French rotated their units through the Verdun battlefield. The units came from all over the war zone, so the Hell that existed in Verdun was shared throughout the entire country. As they patrolled the trenches, battlements and debris covering the walls, many never saw an enemy combatant. Nevertheless, the uncertainty of where the next shell would fall and the unspoken horror of not knowing at what moment he might be blown to bits had a terrifying effect on each man.

Old soldiers, few that there were, had become more inured to the horrors of the battlefield. The young soldiers looked around in numbed shock to see corpses emerge from the entombing mud.

The head-high trenches were evocative of an early grave for the men manning them. The trenches were laid out in parallel lines facing the front as a protection from the artillery barrages. Barbed wire was strung everywhere at the leading edges and beyond to prevent being overrun by the enemy, and machine guns protected the No-Man's- Land, endlessly sweeping their deadly fire back and forth.

The French had defended their land resolutely and finally, in the spring of 1917, there were no shells exploding nor bullets flying.....for the moment at least. The land and the people had paid a great price. In the 39 square miles of the main battle, there were no trees left standing and the fields and the hills in every direction looked like the craters of the moon. The constant hum of the spring hatch of flies was audible, and the awful stench of rotting flesh threatened to evacuate the unprepared stomach. Nature began to take its course as the bodies of horses and oxen and men poked up from the muddy ooze, their decomposition underway.

Winter was finally over and the sun was out. Torn apart by the violence it had received, the thawing ground became a morass of mud, and without the vegetation of the fields and forest to hold it together, it looked more like thick brown pudding. Mud was everywhere. It was a presence. The word, "slog" was invented to describe walking through the quagmire. Suction from the parting ooze tried with all its strength to pull off the loose boot.

A squad of French soldiers was ordered to begin collecting the random body parts lying about. A scarf was wrapped around each of their faces in an attempt to provide at least a psychological barrier from the near-visibly fetid atmosphere. They attempted to keep their handcart from becoming mired in the sludge as they retrieved an arm and shoulder here, a foot there. Identification of the remains was an impossibility and the best they could do was to make an impromptu mass grave in a trench that was collapsing from artillery explosions.

Chapter 1

Lacy James, a pretty and dynamic mother of 4, was supervising the preparations of her family for a well-deserved vacation. School was just out for the summer, and it was finally warming up a bit. She combed her short blonde curls back with her fingers as she surveyed her home. The duplex they lived in was small but comfortable. It had a large back yard that they had planted with a vegetable garden and fruit trees. The garden was growing well, and the apple blossoms had come and gone, replaced with growing apples they would pick in the fall. 11 year-old Allie was at her side helping to pack dishes and food into a covered bin they would take with them on their trip. Lively Allie was not intimidated to be the youngest in the family and was eager to help get them on their way.

The James family lived in Mannheim, Germany in an American housing area called Benjamin Franklin Village. Lacy's husband, Frank, was a Lieutenant Colonel in the US Army, and they had lived in Germany for almost a year. Frank was an engineer and was supervising the "downsizing" of the Army in the Mannheim area. The Army had maintained a presence in Germany since the end of World War II, and the "Powers That Be" had decreed that the time had come for the US military to leave. There were thousands of buildings and hundreds of facilities the Americans had built and maintained throughout Germany since World War II, and Frank's responsibility was the repatriation of those in the Mannheim sector. The facilities each had to be inspected and approved before they were returned to the German government, and he had been working almost non-stop since they had arrived the summer before.

Frank had just turned 41 and was the proud father of 3 sons and a daughter. He maintained a semblance of military discipline in his home, but Lacy was the real authority. When they had named their sons, it seemed balanced, even rhythmic, to have used names beginning with the letter "J". As the boys had grown older and it became more difficult to tell who had done what, he discovered that John, Jarom and Jason were a little hard to separate on his tongue. He found that he was often tripping over the names when he was referring to one or the other of the boys in stressful circumstances.

John, the oldest, had inherited his mother's blonde hair and blue eyes. He was 16, a good student and, wiry and strong, served as captain of the wrestling team at Mannheim American High School. He was currently on top of the family van mounting a cargo carrier that would be used to haul their camping equipment on their upcoming vacation.

Stocky with sandy hair and, sporting the familial blue eyes shared by his siblings, Jarom, 15, was the toughest and wildest of the boys. He was supposed to be helping his brother with packing the van, but was instead high up in the tree that overlooked the carport. With everyone else busy, it seemed like the opportune time to tie a rope high up in the tree. His objective was to take a running start from the roof of the carport, swing out over the yard and around the tree and land atop the garden shed in the back yard.

John wasn't sure where Jarom had gone, but he needed a screwdriver and a pair of pliers that were on the curb next to the van. 13 year-old Jason happened by just in time for a summons from his brother. Tall for his age and thin, with neat dishwater-blonde hair, Jason responded to John's request by handing up the needed tools. He had been on an errand for his mother to retrieve an ice chest from the garden shed and after helping John, he resumed his mission.

Meanwhile, rope in place, Jarom climbed down the tree and out on top of the carport. He grasped the rope in both hands and, with a Tarzan yell and a running take-off, he leapt from the edge of the carport and began the giant circle swing toward the garden shed. Unfortunately, he had forgotten to apprise anyone else of his intentions. Stepping out of the shed with ice chest in hand, and directly in his path was Jason.

John had looked up when Jarom had wailed at the beginning of his swing and, as if it were all happening in slow motion, he could see exactly what the outcome would be. Jarom bowled Jason over as efficiently as if he had been a carefully aimed ball in a bowling alley. The ice chest and both boys went flying across the yard piling up on the side of the garden shed. At first no one moved. John stood up on top of the van for a moment looking for signs of life. Hearing the commotion, Frank looked out the door of the house and followed John's stare to the jumble of bodies against the shed wall. He ran out the door as John jumped to the ground, and both arrived in time to see Jarom smiling. "What a great ride," he said as his eyes rolled back and he went quiet again. There was some movement at the bottom of the heap, and Jason pushed himself from under the pile, Jarom rolling to the side.

All Frank could think was of the possible injuries the boys might have sustained. Back-board, spinal injuries, paralysis, and quadriplegia were all running through his mind, but before he had a chance to do anything, Jarom sat up looking sheepish. Jason started breathing again after having had the wind knocked out of him.

Frank still didn't know what had happened, the rope having swung back out of the way. John explained what had occurred, and by the time Frank began to understand, the boys were looking a bit more normal. Under his breath, he said, "Are you guys OK?"

Jarom and Jason both nodded and, with various grunts and rubs, started to sort out their sundry bruises. Frank said sternly, "Jarom…..That was irresponsible! You were supposed to be helping John with the car carrier. We will discuss this further, but your mother is looking forward to this vacation and we are not, I repeat….ARE NOT, going to ruin it for her before we even start. Do you understand me?"

Jarom answered meekly, "Yes sir", and went on to stand up offering Jason a hand.
Jason took it and stood and, still not having said anything, finally broke his silence. "Wait 'til you find out about payback," he muttered and walked off with the ice chest to the house.

The packing went along a bit more sedately after the "swing" incident. The boys packed their individual gear in their own bags. An air mattress and a sleeping bag for each person was added. The ice chest and tote with the food and dishes, a camping table, two tents, reading material to pass the time, maps and a Michelin Guide, money, tools, cameras, and the myriad other eminently forgettable and often forgotten items were located. Space was allocated, and they were all packed away.

The van was a 3-year-old Ford Transit with two bench seats in the back and a driver's seat and bench seat for two in the front. It had lots of space behind the rear seat for cargo, but for a two-week camping trip, the car carrier was a necessity. By the time everything was loaded, there wasn't much room for anything else. The packing had to be done perfectly to have everything accessible in the correct order for meals during the trip, personal possessions on the way, and camping gear at the end of the day.

Living in Europe was like living in the middle of history. Castles and battlefields, mountain ranges, and lakes and rivers they had heard about their entire lives were there to see. Making time to see them was another matter. It was a major ordeal to organize a trip on this scale despite the fact that another country was less than 100 miles away. Daily life was always in the way. Even though living in Europe was a once-in-a-lifetime experience for Americans, there was still school every day, a job, and normal lives to be lived. Europeans didn't think much about living in the middle of history because they always had. If they went on "Holiday", it was likely to a beach or a resort rather than a moldery old castle or graveyard. The vacation destination for the James family in was France, and the plan was to spend two weeks seeing some of all of the above.

Chapter 2

The plan was to leave bright and early the next morning and so, after an evening of remembering the things they had almost forgotten, they went to bed and woke at 6 AM. A quick breakfast, and they were on the road. Frank and Lacy sat up front with Jarom and Allie in the middle seat and John and Jason in the back. The van was roomy, but it wasn't a powerhouse. With a standard transmission and a two liter engine, it would run only about 140 km/hour at top speed. In American numbers, that was 85miles/hour; faster than most people could legally drive in the United States! It had taken a little while to get used to flying down the road at 85mph, but it was permitted in Germany. As fast as it seemed, the Mercedes and BMWs and Porsches passes the van like it was standing still.

The traffic was always heavy but with no accidents or construction, it moved smoothly. The roads were built for high speeds and the drivers were well-trained and used to driving fast. The rule of the road was, unless you were passing, you stayed in the right lane. This simple rule allowed those that wanted to go fast the ability and kept the trucks and slower vehicles in the right lane where they did not impede the traffic flow. Frank kept the van in the right and center lanes most of the time, watching the rear-view mirror for a headlight flash which indicated someone was coming up quickly from behind.

The first major city they passed through was Kaiserslautern 45 minutes to the southwest. Saarbrucken and the border were about another half hour along, and they had only been traveling a little over an hour when Frank felt a tug on his sleeve.

Allie said, "Daddy, I have to go...."

It was early for a potty stop, but determined to keep the vacation a pleasant one, he said, "OK, honey. We'll stop just over the border."

Since European Unification, there were no more border checks, so Frank had to find an exit from the freeway. Just into

France, he left the freeway and slowed to a stop in front of a small building seemingly built for just the function they required. They all got out of the van to stretch their legs and Allie walked behind the wall facing the road to find what passed for a toilet. She quickly walked back out to the front, and Frank asked, "Done already?"

"Daddy," she said, "I can't go in there...."

"What's the matter?" he asked with a fatherly smile.

"Daddy! There's no toilet!" Frank took her hand, and together they walked behind the divider.

Toilet facilities had been an interesting awakening for the children. Frank and Lacy had seen some of the world and had experienced various bathroom fixtures, but the children had never seen anything except the American standard. In Germany, they were introduced to the "small" flush and the "big" flush; they were informed that gentlemen sit instead of standing over a conventional toilet bowl, and they had used an old-fashioned flush toilet that had a chain-pull to flush and whose bowl was a flat porcelain tray that did not hold water until the flush washed away the waste to the drain at one end. This, however, was a first for Allie. There was just a hole in the floor.

"Honey, you just squat over the hole and everything goes down the drain. You don't sit on anything," assured Frank. This is how more than half of the world uses the toilet. China and Japan and Korea all have toilets without seats. You can do it!" he said as he stepped back around the divider leaving her all alone with the hole.

A few minutes later Allie came back to the front of the screen to the wild applause of her brothers. She turned shades of crimson and ran back to the van. Since they were there, the boys went ahead and used the facility. Frank tried to encourage Lacy to make it a family activity, but she refused saying that she could wait.

Back in the van, Frank and Lacy had planned a stop at the World War I Battleground of Verdun. The children didn't know what Verdun was or the significance of the battle that was fought there. In fact, they were much more eager to continue down the highway to EuroDisney. The road passed Verdun first, however, and after only a few hours from the border they were entering the city itself.

Frank stopped the van at the Citadel in Verdun city. He wanted to have an opportunity to help the children understand what they were about to see, and he was looking for a forum for that explanation. The Citadel had built in the 1620s and was surrounded by a grassy lawn. He herded the family in that direction, and they soon sat comfortably in the grass.

As a senior Army officer, Frank had attended Command and General Staff College and had made a study of the Battle of Verdun. It was of particular importance to him because he was a Combat Engineer by training and profession. The engineering that had gone into the defense of Verdun was awe-inspiring.

After gazing around at the Citadel for a few minutes and not really seeing much, Frank quieted his family, and he began to recite the facts of the World War I battle that had occurred there. At first, the children were restless. They had just been released from confinement in the van and were again being confined in a makeshift classroom. But, as he explained what had happened there, their interest was piqued and they began to ask intelligent questions.

"Verdun has been a crossroads for hundreds of years," he taught. "The Meuse River runs through it from North to South. The main East-West highway passes through, as well as an important North-South highway and a railroad line. Verdun has a population of only about 22,000, and that hasn't changed in 100 years, but the Germans realized its importance. In the Franco-Prussian war in the 1870s, they occupied the position."

John asked, "Dad...that was a long time ago. Why does that matter?"

Frank continued, "The French were determined that Verdun would not be captured again, and as soon as the Germans left in 1873, the French began building a crescent of forts around the city. The first forts were built only a few miles to the east of the city....between it and Germany; and 4 were completed by 1877.

Then, an outer belt of forts was started, and by 1880, about 15 forts surrounded the city."

Jarom was beginning to get interested now. He asked, "That must have made the city really secure! And that was more than 100 years ago!"

"Surprisingly, not as secure as they had hoped," explained Frank. "In 1885, exploding shells were invented and the old forts became almost obsolete. They were outfitted with huge guns that could be aimed in different directions, but the guns were in the open and the concrete of the forts was thin and not reinforced. Direct hits from exploding artillery shells would destroy the guns and the forts, so something else had to be done."

Even Lacy was interested by now, and she asked, "What did they do? Start over again?"

"No", said Frank. "They realized that warfare had changed, but they couldn't discard all of their armaments. They also realized that the area had been overrun repeatedly back as far as Attila the Hun's invasion in the 400s, so history had taught them that they must protect Verdun if they expected to keep it. They began to prepare for a different type of battle by removing some of the guns from the forts and siting them in hidden and protected positons between the big forts. Some of the forts were retrofitted, like Fort Douaumont and Fort Vaux. They had huge steel turrets that could be popped up and were covered with more than 6 feet of reinforced concrete to protect them from the exploding shells. They dug ammunition bunkers, and the gun emplacements were also covered with reinforced concrete to protect them. Then, running between the emplacements, were ditches and barbed wire that the infantry troops could fight from."

John asked, "So they had all those men and guns and ammunition just waiting for the Germans to attack?"

"Yes and no," replied Frank. They were prepared, but not prepared enough. Between 1900 and 1914, they had built 46 armored turrets, 23 bunkers, and 47 armored observation posts. The old forts were all located on the highest ground, so they were both good observation posts as well at good targets. They were used as barracks for the soldiers because they were, more or less, warm and dry."

"So when did the Germans attack them again?" asked Allie. "Wasn't that when the Nazis were fighting with them?"

"No, Sweetie," Frank continued. "That was in the 1930s....World War II. We still haven't got to World War I yet." He smiled at her confusion and went on.

"By 1913, the Germans were attacking to the North in Belgium and were about to come into France. By 1915, things were at a standstill, and they realized that they had to kill the French Army. The Commanding General of the Germans, General Erich von Falkenhayn, knew that Verdun was of great importance to the French, and he knew they would defend it at the expense of all the other fronts. His strategy was not to take Verdun, but to kill as many of the French soldiers as he could so that their Army would be weakened and Germany could then take over the country."

Jason was listening intently, and he caught something from his Dad's explanation that didn't set well with him. "Wait a minute," he said. "Do you mean he just wanted to execute all the soldiers and use Verdun as a trap to draw them in?"

"Exactly," said Frank. "Communications weren't very good in those days, and the Germans began to stockpile huge numbers of guns and shells to the east and north of Verdun, outside of the ring of forts. They built their own bunkers and dug trenches, and they had built an excellent railway system so that they could move their huge guns around and fire them from the trains."

John asked, "Do you mean that the train cars were just big guns?"

"Yes," said Frank. "The Germans, and later the French, both did that. The Germans planned to fire a million shells in the first hours of the battle, and then, after they had incapacitated the French, they would invade with their infantry. On February 21, 1916, the battle began, and in the first 10 hours they fired 1,000,000 shells. Now the Germans were firing at the old forts because that was the obvious thing to do. But, like I said, the French had already moved their guns to better locations. They were hurt badly but were still in the fight. Then the German Infantry attacked; first with flamethrowers that set the French soldiers on fire and then with machine gunners and hand grenades that cleaned up."

"Wow," said Jarom. "Was that the end of the battle?"

"No," replied Frank. "It certainly caused a lot of damage, but they had enough men and munitions that were not where the Germans expected them to be, so they could still fight back. They withdrew where they had to and consolidated their forces. The French fired their artillery back at the Germans from their hidden gun emplacements. The Germans were counting on the forts being a key to the French defeat, but the French weren't in the forts. For instance, in 1916 Fort Douaumont was the most heavily fortified position in the world with its reinforced concrete and guns in turrets. By then, though, the French had realized that a fort was a sitting duck and they had moved most everything out of the fort. There was only a small garrison of a few men in the fort, and the German infantry snuck up to the fort unseen. They couldn't figure out why no one was shooting at them. One of the men crawled in a gun port, and soon a squad of Germans was inside and found no resistance. Finally, they encountered the small garrison eating dinner in a subterranean bunker, and they took over the fort without a shot being fired. This was a huge loss of prestige for the French, but not a loss of military power."

"How did the French keep fighting back? Weren't most of their soldiers killed?" asked Jason.

"They had enough to keep fighting; and remember that the Germans didn't want to take over Verdun. They just wanted to lure in the French soldiers from all over the country and kill them there in their trap. That is what began to happen. The French army sent soldiers from all over the country to fight in Verdun. The Germans originally calculated that they would kill 5 French soldiers for every 2 that they lost, but because the French had been surprisingly well prepared, both sides were losing soldiers at about the same rate, 1:1"

Lacy couldn't hide her shock. "How could they be so cold-blooded as to plan to kill so many of their own soldiers as well as so many of the French? That is just inhumane!"

"Yes, Honey. And that is war. The morale of the men was terrible. The shelling was indescribable. During the 10 months of the battle there were an average of 2 shells per second being fired from one side or the other; morning, noon and night. Having your buddy blown up next to you, and seeing the death and destruction all around was devastating to the men on both sides. The shells that fell on them might have been fired from as far as 25 miles away. From that distance, the shells would rain out of the sky with no warning. The French General recognized the morale problem and he began to rotate divisions in and out of the Verdun area of operations. The German General didn't have that freedom, and his men began to wear down after a while. The British and the Americans were arriving to fight against the Germans on other fronts, but the Germans didn't have reinforcements they could rely on."

"So the Germans started to lose?" asked Allie.

"Yes, Sweetie. That's what happened. The Germans began to retreat and lose the ground they had taken. After 8 months, they occupied almost the same lines that they had when the battle had started. Between February and December of 1916, 24 million shells were fired. An average of 1 death per minute from one side or the other for the entire time. When the Germans finally retreated or surrendered, their Army was demoralized and beaten. The Allies continued to fight on the other fronts, and Germany lost the war."

"Most of the forts are still there after 130 years. All show the scars of the bombardment, and some were completely destroyed so that all that remains are concrete ruins. Many of the bunkers and trenches and tunnels and graves are still there. There are war memorials, and the forest is still there. So....." said Frank, pausing meaningfully "Are you ready to go to EuroDisney?"

"Well, Dad....," said Jarom quickly, having been the most vocal about skipping Verdun and moving on to more exciting destinations, "maybe we could stay a while and see some of the ruins...." The others were nodding and giving their own affirmations.

"OK," said Frank. "If that's the general feeling, let's find a place to camp. Then, we can go and look at some of the sites." The family packed back into the van and Frank headed for a campground he had found on the map. Camping Mairie was located north of Verdun and east of Fort de Vacherauville.

Frank was prone to take back roads when he was either misoriented or exploring. He maintained that he was never misoriented and that exploring back roads was an educational experience. Lacy sometimes had less patience for exploring when she had a destination in mind, but it was still early afternoon and she was willing, so they explored.

Enjoying the beautiful green hills, the farm fields and the sunshine, they turned down a small dirt road. The hills were covered with trees, but one field had some heavy equipment parked in it. It appeared that the equipment was being used to clear the land. There was no one around, and Frank noticed a large concrete block that had been partially uncovered. The block seemed as if it might be interesting, given the history of the area, so he stopped to poke around. The family filed out of the van and Frank began to lead the group into the middle of the field toward the concrete block.

Part way there, Jarom and Jason wandered away from the family to look at the huge excavator and bulldozer that had been working at the site. Before they reached the heavy equipment, they came upon another ruin of disused concrete and stopped to look at it.

Meanwhile, the rest of the family reached the big block and, ever the engineer, Frank wondered aloud about the age of the concrete and the reinforcing steel that was in it. From its remains, he began to piece together what the structure might have originally been. His educated deduction was that it had probably been a bunker for ammunition or supply storage. He guessed that it had been partially destroyed by artillery fire, and he figured the excavator was going to complete the job. The concrete was pockmarked and broken and looked more like eroding granite, but the steel rebar sticking out of the mass was a dead giveaway that it was manmade.

Jarom and Jason began nosing around the other concrete ruin. It could have been the sister to the structure that the rest of the family was looking at, or it may even have been part of the same edifice. Jarom climbed on top to get a better view. The concrete block measured 8 feet high and 20 feet wide; from the top he could see that it was maybe 10 feet deep. He jumped down behind it to find the remains of an old wooden crate pinned underneath.

"Jason," he called. "Come on back here and bring a stick or something to dig with." Jason looked around and saw a piece of rebar sticking out of the broken concrete. It was almost severed with rust and bent at an acute angle. He grabbed hold and as he began to bend it back and forth, it snapped off. Scrambling up to the top of the concrete block, he carried the steel bar to Jarom. He jumped down to where Jarom was, and together they started to dig away the dirt under the crate to free it. The crate must have been nearly 100 years old and came apart immediately. Inside, they found it was full of cans. Jarom pulled one out and looked it over. There was French writing on it, but he didn't read French. He pulled out another, and a third, and soon he and Jason had lined up a dozen of the sealed cans on top of the concrete block. They climbed back on top of the block intending to carry the cans with their unknown contents back to the family.

From the top of the concrete pedestal, they had a commanding view of the field, of their van, and of a truck that had just driven up and stopped. Two men got out of the truck and noticed the boys perched on top of the concrete block. One of them pointed and the other shouted and began to run toward the boys. They were yelling something unintelligible in French and waving their arms.

Jarom and Jason assumed they were in trouble for trespassing. They were accustomed to being in trouble and had plenty of experience. They started to climb down the front of the block. Frank and the rest of the family could hear the commotion, and they began to walk toward the boys when the men got even more excited. Then, Frank saw what Jarom and Jason were holding.

"Jarom, Jason!" he yelled. "Stop and stand still!"

The boys didn't understand what was going on, but they stopped and stood still just as the two men reached them. Ever so gently, one of the men reached out and took one of the cans from Jarom and set it on the block. Then, both men were relieving the boys of their burden and lining the cans up on top of the block. When they had taken all of the cans, they gestured for the boys to move away. Frank and the others arrived, and the men spoke in hurried French, but none of the Americans understood a word. Frank didn't understand the speech, but he understood what the men were trying to convey. It became clear to everyone when one of the men in frustration threw his arms high in the air and to the side while he made an explosion sound with his mouth….,"BOOM!"

Frank said, "You boys have to be CAREFUL out here! You didn't realize that you had picked up a pile of 100 year old hand grenades, but whether you realized it or not, they would blow you up just the same. The explosive in those old things is very unstable after all this time. It might take only a bump to set them off."

The men began to gesture to the family to move back toward the road. On the way, they pointed out a pile of unexploded ordinance they had found while they were working in the field. One of the men went to the truck and came back with a length of fuse, some blasting caps and a small package of plastic explosive. He put one cap in the pile of ordinance and the other in the middle of the cans the boys had found and then ran the fuses out 5 or 6 feet.

Frank gathered that it must be common for earthmovers in the area to find "duds" and other explosives when they were clearing an old field. He said, "I read that, by conservative estimates, there are 1 million explosives still in the battle area. Maybe we should have had that lesson earlier!"

While the men were getting ready, the family walked back to where the van and the truck were parked; 75 or 100 yards away. One of the Frenchmen motioned for Frank to follow him as he drove his truck another 100 yards away. The other workman remained with the explosives. He pulled out his matches and lit the fuses and started to run to the truck. The fuses were slow burning, so he had plenty of time. The driver motioned for them to all get behind the vehicles to watch.

The thunder and concussive force of a violent explosion rolled over the cleared land. They saw smoke and dirt fly up in the air and felt the impact of the sound waves penetrating their bodies, but they were far enough away to escape being covered with debris. It was clear that the men had done this before, and both the Frenchmen laughed as the Americans looked on with wonder on their faces.

They signed their thanks to the men and loaded back into the van intending to go on to the campground. Frank consulted his map and concluded that they were in the vicinity of Ouvrage de Froideterre in the Fleury Woods. The Ouvrage was a mini-fort near the town of Fleury, and Fleury was infamous for having changed hands 16 times in 3 months during the heaviest fighting. The town had finally been completely obliterated, and the area around it had been overrun by both armies repeatedly. Frank, unable to resist another small road, turned down a track through the woods overgrown with weeds and brush. The branches scratched unmercifully against the sides of the van and made sounds like a cat yowling in discontent. Lacy protested to Frank, "How are we going to get out of here? You'll have to back up down this path again!"

As Frank began to wonder if he had, indeed, made a mistake, the van entered a clearing that fronted on a large stone arch buried in the side of a hill. The top of the hill over the arch was covered with grass and foliage that had grown up over it so there appeared to be a continuous forest floor from both sides of the 30 foot arch up the top. Behind them, extending out through the woods in opposite directions and perpendicular to the track they had driven in on, meandered an overgrown linear depression. The ground was cratered on all sides with trees growing up from the depths of the craters and the ridges between them.

"Imagine what this would look like with no trees or bushes or grass growing here," Frank posed. "The ground would be covered with bomb craters on all sides so that everything alive would have been destroyed, and the earth would have looked like the craters in the surface of the moon." Everyone was lost in their own thoughts as they looked out through the trees and at the broken forest floor.

John said, "Wow….the explosions must have been unbelievable to have killed all the trees and everything. How long did it take everything to grow up again?"

Frank replied, "I read that the Forestiers replanted the woods in the 1930s, but the bomb craters still remain. You can imagine that in the 80 years since then, trees might have grown up and died and new ones might have grown up again. This bunker in front of us must have been a target as well as a refuge for one or both sides as the area was taken and retaken repeatedly. Shall we get out and take a look?"

"No!" said Lacy. "Let's go find the campground. We can come back here tomorrow, but I want to get our camp set up before dark, and it's getting late."

"I was thinking that we could just camp here," said Frank mildly. "There's no traffic here and we would be undisturbed. It would be perfect!"

"There's no bathroom here, Daddy!" chimed in Allie.

"That's right, Frank," added her mother.

"We don't need a bathroom," said Frank. "We can just use the woods."

"Maybe you soldiers can use the woods," she said, "but we want a bathroom!" said his wife.

Frank could see that it was a losing battle. They might return to the subject later, but for now, he could accept defeat. He smiled and took out his GPS and marked the spot so they could find their way back. There was an opening under the arch, and the boys were already getting excited to explore the inside of the bunker.

"Did you guys bring your headlamps?" asked their father.

"Of course!" they chorused. They had learned the value of their headlamps in their underground adventure in Mannheim, and they didn't travel without them.

"Good!" said Frank. "It looks like they'll come in handy when we come back."

Frank turned the van around in the small clearing in front of the archway and scraped their way back down the mud track and out onto the road.

"There must be dozens and dozens of old bunkers and stuff around here," said Jarom, looking at the map. There are a few on the map, so exploring the little roads like this might lead us to more of them."

All the children were enthused about exploration of the old ruins. EuroDisney suddenly became much less important.

Chapter 3

  Frank pulled the van back out onto the road and then, with directions from Lacy and a little help from the map, they made their way to Camping Mairie. They turned into the campground and parked at reception while Frank and John went in to rent a space. The attendant spoke passable English and they were given a spot near the pool and the bathroom which they decided was a double-win. Frank drove to the space only to find that someone else had parked partly in their slot and had left lawn chairs occupying the rest of it. Frank got out of the van and walked over to the camping trailer that was invading his space. He knocked on the door and got no answer. A moment passed and he knocked again. Finally a man opened the door a crack. Frank said politely, "Excuse me, but you're parked in our spot and we need to pull in. Could you please move your trailer?"

  The man opened the door a little wider and looked at Frank, waved his hand, and closed the door. Unsure of the meaning of the exchange, Frank waited a few moments for the man to return but, when he didn't come back to the door, Frank pounded a bit harder. The man finally returned and opened the door. He spoke angrily in French and Frank began pointing at the space he was supposed to occupy and trying to make himself understood by speaking louder and more slowly.

  Soon the altercation was in danger of becoming violent with neither man apparently understanding the other or being willing to back down. Finally, the "neighbor" in the space on the other side of the street stuck his head out of his own camper and asked in accented English, "Vat seems to be the problem?" Both Frank and the other man turned to him and after a short pause, began to present their multilanguage cases to him. The bilingual man soon understood the problem. He explained to the hostile Frenchman that his trailer and equipment were encroaching upon Frank's space and the man settled down. It seemed that he thought Frank wanted him to move out of his own space and he refused to budge.

Finally, he unhappily pulled the blocks from around the wheels of his trailer and, after pulling it forward, backed it in properly. The boys had gathered up the armchairs and brought them back to their owner who took them ungraciously. They went to their own space and waited while Frank turned to talk to the intermediary.

"My name is Frank James," he said as he introduced himself and reached out his hand to shake. The linguist shook hands and said, "Hello. My name is Francois Petain," he said. "I am pleased to meet you."

"Thank you very much for intervening on our behalf," said Frank. Francois looked puzzled. "For helping us," he simplified.

"Oh. It is nothing," replied Francois.

By this time the unpleasant man had re-chocked his wheels and disappeared inside the trailer.

"Sometimes my countrymen are impatient with the, how do you say, tourists."

"Well, I am very grateful for your help. My family and I are here to see the battlefields of Verdun. I couldn't help noticing your last name. Are you related to General Petain?"

The man smiled somewhat ruefully. "Yes. I am his great-grandson. Verdun was his finest hour, I am afraid. He had many hours later that were not as fine."

Frank understood what he meant. General Petain had commanded the Armies at Verdun and had prevailed but had made some very poor decisions in World War II that had ruined his reputation.

Frank said, "Well, I had better pull into our space and get our camp set up. Perhaps we can talk later?"

"Of course," said Francois. "I will look forward to it."

He went back over to the van and pulled it into the space he had reserved. John climbed up on the roof and opened up the clamshell car carrier. He began tossing down the tent poles and sleeping bags while Jason and Jarom opened the rear hatch and began unloading the back. Lacy directed them to put the tote with the food on the picnic table and then the boys began to set up the tents.

Setting up the tents was a task they had perfected. They had done it many times on family campouts, in their own back yard, and even on Boy Scout campouts. One tent was a canvas wall tent with a waterproof bottom and a theoretically waterproof top. The other was a large dome tent that their parents claimed as a refuge from the children at days end. Allie was old enough to not have to sleep with Mom and Dad, so she had begun to claim her quarter of the big tent.

They lay the tent down on the ground and pounded in the stakes at each one of the guy lines. Then they assembled the ridge pole and slid it through the canvas top. Finally, they attached a vertical pole to each end of the ridge pole and with one of the older boys on each of the two legs, they uprighted the tent and held it in position while Allie and Jason fastened, and then tightened, the guy lines. Each of the children claimed their corner and then set about blowing up the air mattresses and laying out their sleeping bags.

Their day had hardly been strenuous, but traveling had at least made them hungry. Lacy, who had been cooking their dinner at the picnic table, called for them to get out the paper plates and plastic ware. They complied while she finished assembling the food. Her general preference was to see how nice a meal she could cook in a camping environment, but tonight she settled for preparing the meal quickly. She made the children's favorite-Macaroni and Cheese-which she customized with some sautéed onions and sausage slices. Fresh, ripe peaches were dessert, and a loaf of French bread was sliced and served with garlic and butter. The family gathered around the picnic table and prepared to eat. Frank asked Allie to bless the food, which she did, and they all dug in hungrily.

After dinner, Francois came out of his trailer and he sat at his own picnic table. Frank rose and asked him if he would like to join them. He companionably crossed to their table and sat down. Frank had told the family during dinner that Francois was the great-grandson of General Petain. He had explained who the General had been, and they were interested to see if Francois had any insights into Verdun. Lacy offered them all some candies and Francois took one.

Without preamble, Jarom asked Francois if he knew the battleground, and Francois began to talk.

"I did not know my Great-Grandfather. He had died before I was born, but I heard the stories from my father about the war. We actually lived in a village a few miles south on the Meuse called Bannoncourt, so I knew the area well. The shelling during the battle had destroyed the woods all around so, when I was a boy, the trees that had been planted to restore the area were small. It was common to find many artifacts that were lost in the war. Imagine the millions of shells that exploded in this very area! The men and equipment were blown up and we would find cartridges and coins and parts of the soldiers uniforms scattered all over, left only to the forest."

Francois was about 60 years old. His hair had grayed and he had some of the creases of age in his face but was otherwise trim and healthy as if he had spent much of his life outdoors. He was very congenial and seemed eager to share his memories.

"Sometimes, as children walking through the woods, we would find a bone or a tooth, but my father used to tell us that when he was a child after the Great War they would often find bones. He said that the Forestiers would pull a cart through the woods as they were planting trees to collect the bones of the arms and the legs and sometimes even the skulls that had been lost in the mud and buried during the war."

"The old forts became our secret places. They had no purpose, really, and most were badly damaged. Some were completely destroyed and unrecognizable. There were tunnels, sometimes more than a mile long, that connected bunkers and barracks and forts together in an area. The trenches were still there, and the barbed wire was still strung, in many places, from post to post. We would run in the trenches and play hide-and-seek. It probably did not show proper respect for the soldiers, but we were children and this was part of our home."

"Are there still tunnels and underground rooms here?" blurted Jarom. He was thinking of his own experiences in tunnels back in Mannheim and was eager to see more.

"Yes. Of Course. Because some of the unreinforced tunnels collapsed, they are no longer accessible, but I remember where some of the best forts were. Would you like to see them?"

The children's excitement was unrestrained and Frank looked quite interested. Lacy was more hesitant. Her past experience in tunnels had taught her to be wary of them, and she wasn't happy to see her offspring off on another underground adventure.

She said, "I don't know if we should be poking around underground….."

John jumped in, "Mom, Francois is like a professional guide. He knows this area!"

"I'm sorry, Mrs. James, if I have made you uncomfortable. I am here doing what you are doing. I am visiting the old battlefields that I grew up around. I haven't been here in many years and I wanted to relive some of the memories of my youth, if you understand. I assure you that I have no intention of placing your children or myself in any danger."

Frank quickly added, "I think we can keep the kids on a short leash, honey. And you can come too! It will be fascinating!"

"Well……I suppose the children will be OK with a guide, but I'll have to think more about whether or not I want to come," said Lacy.

Jason piped in, "I knew we would finds some cool things here. I brought my head lamp and everything, and so did John and Jarom."

Allie admitted, "I did too. I thought I might need a flashlight so I brought it along."

Then Frank laughed, "I brought yours and mine too, sweetheart. I think this must be fate!"

They talked a while longer, but it was well past dark, and everyone was getting tired. They arranged to meet Francois in the morning after breakfast at about 8 AM. They thanked him for his help and his stories, and he went back to his trailer while the James family retired to their own tents.

Frank and Lacy zipped up the door of their tent and, in low tones, began to discuss the day.

"Frank, I get the feeling that you didn't plan to just be a typical tourist here. I think you were planning just the sort of excursion that Francois described! If I didn't know any better, I would think that you had prearranged this with him. You know that those tunnels frighten me!"

He tried to comfort his agitated wife. "Lacy, I'm an engineer. I studied this battlefield at Command and General Staff College and I wrote a paper on it. This is the fulfillment of a professional dream, and I AM excited that my family can join me. Finding Francois to guide us is such a bonus; I can't refuse. I promise! I'll take care of the kids if you don't want to come along; if you do, then you can watch over them too."

Mollified and somewhat abashed, she turned to her husband and said, "Fine. Have fun. Don't let them get in trouble or get hurt. I might even come too, but I'm going to sleep on it." And with that, she crawled into her sleeping bag and moved as far away on the air mattress as its size would allow.

Chapter 4

The orange ball of the sun shone through a cloudless sky the next morning as the James family excitedly awoke. The promise of exploring long-forgotten forts and buried tunnels aroused the archeological instincts of Frank and the kids. Lacy would have been better described as agitated. She wanted to enjoy her family's enthusiasm, but her own suppressed claustrophobia, and the memories of the dangers that her brood had faced in earlier times damped the enthusiasm she otherwise might have felt.

Several months before, her children had discovered a tunnel under the military housing area they where they lived in Germany. They had discovered both stolen Nazi treasures and a death room where those that built the tunnels had been permanently entombed. Jarom had been poisoned and all had been threatened during the adventure, so her reticence was understandable. Nevertheless, she tried to be an understanding mother and wife; she put on an upbeat expression and supervised the frying of eggs and bacon and the cutting of melons for breakfast.

After the meal, Francois emerged from his camp trailer and crossed the open space between them.

"Good morning," he greeted them.

The family returned his salutations with their own and invited him to sit at the table.

"I'm afraid the bacon and eggs are gone, Francois, but would you join us for some honeydew melon?" asked Lacy.

He accepted her offer, and they began to discuss their plans for the day.

"You have not seen anything yet?" he asked.

Frank replied that they had stopped at the citadel briefly the day before and described their encounter with the hand grenades. He also mentioned that they had traveled down the dirt track into the woods and had found the bunker entrance, but they had not gone in as yet.

"Well, it sounds as if you have had an introduction to what the people here have been living with for 100 years. May I suggest that we start the day at the Douaumont Ossuary; then we can look at Fort Souville? These are the places that all of the tourists that come here visit, and they give a good overview of what the war was like. Then, we can experience a more private tour of some of the places that the tourists never see," proposed Francois.

Lacy immediately replied for the group, "That sounds great to us!" She thought that the more time they spent on the established tourist trail, the less they might spend in a tunnel somewhere.

They all pitched in putting away the food and securing their belongings as best they could in an open campsite. Francois' car was hitched to his camping trailer, so Frank asked, "Would you like to ride with us, Francois? We have plenty of room, and we're eager to hear what you have to share."

Francois agreed, and with Frank in the driver's seat and Francois riding shotgun, the family piled in the back and they left the campground. Because they had a "local" leading the expedition, there was no need for a map, and Francois guided Frank over the roads. Soon, in the distance, they could see a four-sided stone tower that rose vertically from the cross of an inverted, three armed T-shaped base; the arms of which were set at 90 degrees to each other. The fourth and front side presented a long, straight, tubular building strangely resembling the body of a submarine. The tower contained a bell, and Francois told them it was referred to as the Death Bell. It was rung at official ceremonies. A continuously burning light shone out over the graves and was referred to as the Death Lantern. At the front of the monument was a vast cemetery covered with thousands of evenly spaced crosses. Francois told them that it contained over 16,000 graves and that it was the largest single French cemetery of the First World War. It contained the remains of both French and German soldiers, and they read on a sign as they pulled in that the ossuary was built in the 1920s and finished in 1932.

Frank parked the van and reminded the children that this was a place deserving of their respect and silence, and they quietly walked up to the building. Inside, they found long hallways that extended out opposite one another. The hallways were divided into 18 alcoves, each of which contained a pair of tombs. They read on an information brochure they picked up at the entrance that the tombs held the bodies of men that were found on particular areas of the battlefield, and two immensely larger tombs held the overflow. The total volume of all of the tombs inside was almost 1,000 cubic meters. Each brick on the interior wall was inscribed with the name of a fallen soldier, but there were far too few bricks to name them all.

The third arm of the "T" contained a war museum that housed viewers for glass slides of photographs that were taken during and after the war. They spent some time flipping through the slides which gave them a graphic picture of the death and destruction that was Verdun in World War I. When they had been through the museum, Francois suggested that they walk around the outside of the memorial. The solemn mood prevailed, and as they reached the end of one of the arms of the "T" and rounded the corner, they began walking up the back side of the arm which, at first, seemed far less ornate and decorated than did the front. As they walked, they noticed the large windows that were framed into the massive walls, and they looked through the windows with unbelief. There, inside the chamber behind each window, lay the skeletal fragments of those whose bodies were not intact on the battlefield and could not therefore be identified. One window might have looked into a vault containing only arm bones, stacked like firewood. The next might have contained leg bones and the next skulls. Altogether, the remains of 130,000 soldiers rested in the ossuary.

As they walked back to car through the graves, the attitude of solemnity continued, and no one spoke until they were assembled back in the van. Francois said, "I wanted you to feel the magnitude of the destruction. Talking about incomprehensible numbers does not show what the photographs and graves do. I believe you feel the reverence we French have for Verdun and the symbol that it is for us; of the tremendous sacrifice the people of our nation made in the Great War. Now, if you desire, I would like to take you the Verdun Memorial Museum."

Frank said, "Francois, you are so generous with your time and your knowledge that we could not refuse. We are grateful and want to continue the tour as you have planned it." The various family members all nodded their agreement, and Frank started the engine. With Francois' direction, he drove toward the museum.

On the way, Francois continued to speak, saying, "The museum is built on the site of the train station of the original town of Fleury. The town was in the center of the battle and was completely destroyed. It was as far as the Germans ever advanced during the battle, and it was taken and retaken many times by both sides. The Museum was built in 1967 to educate our children and others about the Battle of Verdun. The museum has two levels inside. On the upper level you will find the uniforms, weapons, ammunition, and the tools that were in use during the war. Also from the upper level, you have a view of the lower level which is a reconstructed trench that the infantrymen fought from. You will see the barbed wire and representations of the difficulties they faced, such as the mud, thirst, hunger and fleas; not to mention the constant threat of explosions which might immediately kill or bury them. There are several films you may watch to get a feeling of the actual battle. "

Frank and Lacy and their children looked immensely interested, so Francois continued as if he were a practiced tour guide.

"This road we are driving on," he continued, "is part of the Voie Sacree, or in English, the Sacred Way. In 1916 however, it was thought more of as the Road to Hell because along this road, all of the supplies and ammunition, as well as all of the soldiers, had to pass. The traffic was continuous, night and day. General Petain only kept units on the front lines for a few weeks at a time, rotating in others from all over the country. More soldiers fought at Verdun than anywhere else in France. The terror of non-stop bombardment was shared widely, but it was shared among more men, so the strain on each man was less. As a result of the rotation of the troops, 1/3 of all the soldiers in France served at one time or another in Verdun. The Germans kept the same units on the line until they were destroyed, and their morale was terrible."

"The museum is just ahead, but see the markers on the side of the road, each with a French soldier's helmet on it? Those are the markers of the Voie Sacree."

Frank parked the van and they piled out; Francois stopped them for a moment.

"There were 13 villages in the bombardment area that no longer exist. Fleury is in the middle of them. The bombardment was so severe that the buildings were completely destroyed. The bomb craters were everywhere and the soil was poisoned by all of the metal from the shells. Arial photography from 1917 and 1918 showed no trace of the original villages. The people could not rebuild their towns, and the French government bought up the land for a memorial. As you found out yesterday, shells continue to rise to the surface of the fields which makes working the land dangerous, even after 100 years."

They looked out over what appeared to be pleasant rolling hills dotted with small trees. The hills, though, were actually formed from earth blown out of the bomb craters by the explosions.

They entered the museum and immediately saw the trench. As they stood close, they heard a simulation of the continuous explosions of artillery shells that must have terrified the soldiers. Barbed wire lined the border between the trench and the No-Mans-Land. Steel supports, made of round 5/8" rod, were driven in the ground with loops bent into them at three heights. Barbed wire strung through the loops created a fence. They could see the simulation of soldiers eating and sleeping and firing their weapons, and of a command post in the trench. Part of the trench had caved in as if an artillery shell had burst upon it. The men were filthy, tired, and covered in mud.

Individually, they wandered around the museum and, after spending time looking at the displays and watching the silent movies, they gathered outside to discuss the rest of the day.

Lacy pointed out, "It's about noon and we haven't any food here. I thought there might be a café, but apparently there are none. Shall we just go back to the camp and eat lunch before we go out for the afternoon?"

Francois said, "You are correct. There are no restaurants around here and it is not far to the camp. Why don't we eat lunch? Then this afternoon, I have even more interesting things to show you. Lacy shivered involuntarily and they all got back in the van.

Frank chauffeured the group back the way they had come, and in a short while they were at the camp. When they pulled up, they saw that their tents had been knocked down, their bags had been opened, and their dishes spilled on the ground. There had been nothing of real value left behind, and it didn't appear that anything was missing, but they were understandably upset.

Jarom angrily pointed at the trailer next door and said, "I bet it was the guy that was parked in our place yesterday. We should go over there...."

Frank turned to him and said brusquely, "Jarom, we have no evidence of that. It is more likely that thieves were looking for something valuable and were disappointed we left nothing behind to steal, so they just trashed the tents. Keep your thoughts to yourself for now, and let's get the tents back up again. Then we can eat."

Francois declined the invitation to join them and returned to his own camp trailer.

John watched him go and said, "I hope we're not wearing him out."

Jarom added, "What he showed us this morning was really interesting, but I want to see the old forts."

Lacy replied, "I'm sure he just wants to leave us alone for a while. He seems to be truly enjoying his role as our tour guide. We really couldn't have been luckier in finding him"

While the others cleaned up the camp, Allie and Jason picked up the tote and refilled it with the dishes. Lacy got out a loaf of bread, sandwich meat, lettuce, tomato, and mayonnaise and everyone made his own sandwich. The boys were done eating almost before anyone else had started, so Jarom opened the back of the van and found the football he had tucked in under the bags. The other boys spread out and they started to pass the ball around. They had only been throwing a few minutes when Jason missed a pass and the ball flew on to bounce off the side of their grumpy neighbor's trailer. Jason retrieved the ball and they held their collective breaths, but the door opened and the man came out speaking loudly in French. They weren't sure what to do because it didn't appear that he could understand them, and their attempt at apology was not acknowledged.

Hearing the racket, Francois stepped out of his trailer and quickly understood what had happened.

John asked, "Could you please tell him we are sorry we hit his trailer with the ball. We won't let it happen again."

Francois spoke with the man in French, and the man seemed mollified, finally turning away. With a few final words, he went back inside. Francois shrugged his shoulders as if to say that the man would likely never be happy.

Chapter 5

"I think this afternoon that we will go and see one of the forts that was nearly destroyed by the shelling, "said Francois, as they all got back into the van. He directed Frank to drive to the south and west, and in a very few minutes they were driving on a road with farm fields on either side. There were no signs of any military installations in the area, and Francois had to watch carefully because he had not been there for some time.

"Slow down here, Frank," he said. I think we will want to turn on this farm road." The land really was rolling hills and not just bomb craters. At Francois's direction, Frank started down a rough dirt road that led up a hill covered with trees. The hill was too steep to farm and was not cultivated. Trees and vines grew up wildly, and yet the rudimentary mud track continued.

Lacy noticed wild fruit trees growing along the track. She pointed out cherries and apples that would be ripe in another few months. The continued climbing along the old trail until they came to a tall chain-link fence with old rusty signs on the gate. Frank parked the van and the troop got out.

"When I was a young man, we would come up in the fall and eat the cherries and the apples that grew on this hillside. The farms around here were not well developed at the time. I suspect that because we are at the outer perimeter of the ring of forts and west of Verdun, there was less shelling here so the land was salvageable. Beyond this fence though, nothing has happened in 100 years. It is a good example of the land being left to itself without any contribution from men."

Jason pointed out, "The road looks like it gets used; but with the gate locked, where does anyone go?"

Frank laughed and said, "Roads to nowhere get double the traffic because everyone travels them twice."

Francois continued, "If we walk through the woods to the right, we should find a hole in the fence." After a pause, he said, "The old forts actually still belong to the French Army, but there is no reason for them to maintain them or guard them. They are seldom visited because, these days, they are only known by a few, and there is nothing of value in them anyway. They are only curiosities"

He led them off through the heavy woods, and, after walking a few hundred yards along the perimeter fence, they came upon a breach in the fence. They each had to get down on hands and knees and worm-crawl under the fencing as another held up its edge; but in short order they were all inside.

There was still no sign of a fort, and they began walking up the hill through increasingly thick vegetation. The regularly spaced trees that had been planted by the Forestiers in the 1930's in the other woods they had seen were missing. The ground was a tangle of vines and bushes and trees, alive and dead. There was little else to see because the woods were so dense, but, after 15 minutes of walking, there appeared the outline of a huge concrete construction. The concrete had been badly damaged and was broken in many places. There were bushes and trees growing out of cracks where the surface had been broken or where soil had collected over the years, and it was clearly a ruin that had been abandoned long-ago.

The boys ran ahead of the group and scrambled down to the bottom of a deep ditch that surrounded the entire fort. Much to their mother's consternation they were off circling the fort looking for an entrance. Soon, they were shouting back to the slower moving adults and their sister that they had found a "window" into the fort. A few minutes later, the rest of the company had joined them in the ditch.

"Why is this big ditch here?" wondered Jarom aloud.

Frank answered, "This is a moat. It's just like a moat surrounding one of the castles we've visited or that you've seen in the movies. And see the steel doors above us? A drawbridge was probably constructed there to limit access to the fort, even though it has likely been gone for some time." Pointing at the walls, he continued, "The openings along the fort walls are firing ports where soldiers would have been stationed to protect the fort from anyone trying to cross the moat."

John asked, "Isn't that like the firing ports on castles we've seen?"

"Yes," said his father, "except those were shaped for bows. They were taller but, like these, shaped so that they are wider on the inside to allow the soldiers to aim to the left or the right, but with a narrow opening to the outside to minimize their target value."

The outside of the fort consisted of a wall that stood about 20 feet high facing the moat. It was no casual construction and was made entirely of stone and block set in mortar. The walls were feet thick, and Francois walked down the moat a bit to where the wall had collapsed and pointed up to a gap above where there was a rockslide.

He said, "I think we can climb up that rubble and then up the broken part of the wall to the top." The boys scrambled eagerly up the side, and Allie followed closely. After they had reached the top and looked down, they discovered that there wasn't much to see. John and Jarom went back to where their mother was climbing up the broken wall and grabbed her hands to help her up. Finally Frank and Francois ascended to the top where the boys were already looking around. There was a huge round steel circle set in the concrete with a large hole in the center. They were peering down into it when the rest of the party joined them.

John said, "I bet this is where one of the cannons was mounted!"

Francois agreed, saying, "Yes. The forts were arranged in a circle around the city to protect it, and the gun that was mounted here could be rotated in any direction so that it could be aimed at the threat. You see the geared steel track surrounding the hole? It was used to turn the entire turret that held the gun."

"This fort is Fort de Choisel, and it was situated to repel an invasion from the north if the Germans were to bypass the most direct route through Verdun in favor of a flanking movement through Belgium, for instance."

Jason asked, "Well, where's the fort? All there is here are a couple of bumps sticking up and a small building on both ends."

"You are right, Jason," said Francois. "There is not much to see here because most of the fort is underground. The two "buildings" you see are actually late additions to the fort. They are called Bourges Casemates, which were reinforced concrete and steel emplacement of 75mm. artillery pieces. There is a lot plant growth here that has occurred over the past 100 years, but look at this wall and you will see a sort of window."

They crossed to the wall, and he suggested that it was time to put on the headlamps. With lights blazing from each forehead, they crawled through the window aperture on their bellies, but the window was high in the wall from the inside and they had to drop 5 feet to the ground. John was the first in with Jarom and Jason following. Gentlemen that they were, they helped Allie and their mother stretch to reach the ground. The men were able to slide in on their own. With the window, the room wasn't dark, but it was the only opening to the outside.

To orient them, Francois said, "This level was not heavily reinforced. It would have been used in peacetime as a barracks block when the soldiers lived here, but there was no immediate threat of attack."

They noticed that the ceilings were arched and that each doorway and window had an arch for support of the wall over it. At soon as their eyes had adjusted to the dim light, they began to appreciate how vast the fort must be. The walls were either brick, block and mortar, or poured concrete. They filed out of the room they had entered through and came to a hallway. The hallway extended maybe 75 or 100 yards in either direction, and, as they began to walk along the hallway, they could see the same room built over and over. A latrine room could be entered off the hallway, and at the end of the hallway was a set of stairs that steeply descended to the next level down.

Francois directed them to take the stairs down, and, as they did, they noticed the walls were smooth, and that there was a red line about 4 inches wide extending in each direction halfway up the wall. Jarom asked Francois what the significance of the red line was, and he said, "The red line indicates that the ceiling and walls are 'bombardment-proof', made of poured and reinforced concrete several feet thick. When there was a threat the alarm would be sounded, and each person would report to his assigned post to guard a firing port, to be a sentry, to crew one of the 75mm. guns, or to man the machine guns."

The whole underground level they were on was constructed of reinforced concrete, and, as they began to walk in the corridors on the first underground level where no light was filtering in from above, their headlamps became of prime importance. They moved along the corridor and could see light coming from a passage that extended toward its middle. They followed the light to its source and looked up at the remains of the 75mm. cannon foundation they had seen from the top of the fort. The gun itself had been long ago removed, but the mangled beams of steel and broken cement bore witness to the explosive shell that had destroyed the big gun. They noticed, from the bottom, the geared ring they had seen from above that allowed the gun to turn. They could also see the remains of a steel track that went around corners in the corridor and extended into another room.

Jarom asked, "Was that track to move the ammunition from the storage room to the gun?"

"Good guess, Jarom!" said his father. "The storage room, or magazine, was in a highly fortified place because an explosion there might destroy the whole fort. To move the heavy shells, they would suspend them from a trolley that ran on that rail and push them along to the gun where they would be loaded by hand. It probably took at least two men to handle one of those big shells, and cannons in some of the forts used 155mm. shells; more than twice as large as the ones used here."

After they had inspected the destroyed gun emplacement, they came to the rusty remains of another steel support structure. Francois told them that it was the bottom compartment of a machine gun turret. He added, "Both the cannons and the machine gun turrets were covered with a flat-top steel cover that could be raised by use of a counterweight system in the shaft. The cover over the machine gun is down, and the one over the cannon was destroyed during the battle. There was also an observatory to view the circumstances outside and control the fire of the guns. There was one on each end of the fort covered with a 7"steel cap, both of which were destroyed."

"After the 'Great War', he continued, "It was recognized that their needed to be interconnecting tunnels between the forts, as well as within the forts, to allow resupply, reinforcement, and escape. Fort Vaux, one of the forts at the battle's front, was attacked by the Germans, and the French held out inside until they were forced to surrender; not because they were out of ammunition or that they were overrun, but because they ran out of water. A deeper network of interconnecting tunnels would have prevented that. The work was started in 1917 but was never completed. The tunnel system was called "Travaux 17", which translates to "Works 17"

"The reason this fort is in such excellent condition is that it saw very little action. It was far from the battle's front line, and, while it received fire, it didn't receive nearly as much as the forts to the east."

The boys had listened interestedly, but the pace the adults had set was getting boring. There was still lots to look at, and they could see signs that soon they would be directed back to the van. The three boys looked at each other, wordlessly communicating their intent, and then John said, "Dad, we want to go have a look at the last stairway we passed."

Frank looked at Francois who shrugged his shoulders and said, "There is only one way out. They have but to go up."

He nodded his permission and then said, "OK, but you kids stay together; and let's check our watches right now. It's 3:30. We will see you on top of the fort at 4:15."

The boys took off at a run. They ran back to the last set of stairs and started down. The further down they went, the darker it got. There was no communication to the top through the old gun-shafts for light to filter through. They came to another level that consisted of more barrack rooms, and they found the cesspit where the human waste dropped down from the level above. There was also a huge concrete tank that they supposed was the water supply for the fort.

Finally, they came to another stairway that looked incomplete; more roughly hewn into the natural stone and not completely reinforced. Jarom asked, "The Travaux 17 tunnels?"

John agreed, "I think you're right," and they started to pick their way through the passage.

Jason said, "Do you think it's safe to go on through here?"

Jarom shot back, "These tunnel have been here for 100 years. They aren't going choose this moment to collapse."

Jason was mollified and they continued deeper into the earth.

A few more minutes went by, and John said, "It's hard to guess where this tunnel goes, but we don't have much time to explore it. We have come down a lot, and we've been going in a straight line for most of the way. We must be under the moat by now."

They kept walking along the tunnel in single file; the tunnel wasn't big enough to walk side-by-side, and, even with their lights massed together, they couldn't see the end. They came to an intersection where the tunnel forked right and left. Not wanting to get lost, they agreed to take the left fork.

Pointing to the right, Jarom proposed, "Maybe that one goes to the next fort in the line that way."

"Could be," said John.

They proceeded until they came to another staircase that was headed up. They started to climb the staircase which consisted of several runs of about 20 steps. Finally, they could actually see light through, what appeared to be, a round hole in the roof. The stairs became a spiral staircase, then, made from rusted steel, and the walls were round as if they were climbing up through a cylinder. The higher they went, the slicker and more wet the stairs became. There was slime growing on them, and they had to be careful not to fall, though the steps seemed sturdy enough.

As it turned out, they *were* climbing up through a cylinder. When they came to the top, there was a platform that extended around the perimeter of the opening to the sky. A huge steel cap once covered the opening, but it had been knocked off and now rested on the ground at the base of the tower they were standing on.

The view would have been panoramic if not for the trees that had grown up on all sides. Some of the tree branches almost scraped against the side of the stone tower.

John said, "This must have been an observation post. From here, there would have been a great view of the whole valley. Someone from here could have told the people in the fort where an attack might have been coming from, and at the edge of the woods like this, would not have been visible to the attackers."

"But how would they have communicated? "asked Jarom. "They didn't have radios, did they?"

"Well, not wireless radios," said John. "But they had wired radios. There have been some insulators here and there that wire used to be strung on. I read back at the museum that there was wired communication from each of the forts back to the citadel in Verdun. That way, the commander in the citadel could control the battle and inform the different fort commanders of what was happening. Imagine the priority it must have been for the enemy to cut the wires or to intercept the communication by tapping into them! I suppose they could have had similar communications from here."

Jarom looked at his watch. "4:00," he noted.

They started back down the stairs and began to walk along the tunnel again. It was late and they didn't want their father upset at them so they started to jog along the tunnel. It was clearly not finished and hadn't existed during World War I. They saw the continuation of the passage go on straight ahead as their turn appeared on their right. It was the right fork they had seen on their way in, but they didn't even slow down for it as they turned toward the fort and kept going. They slowed a bit as they came to a more broken-down part of the tunnel and looked at the ceiling more closely. They noticed that, in places, the only supports for the ceiling were rotting wooden posts instead of concrete reinforcement. Resuming their pace, Jason, at the end of the line, bumped one of the posts. It was weak enough that it could not withstand even the small lateral force of the "bump" and, with weight on it from above, broke in half. The ceiling it was supporting creaked and began to fall in behind them. They couldn't tell the extent of the cave in, but ran like crazy on into the fort and safety. Dirt flooded out of the tunnel and the displaced air pushed them along. They climbed back up the stairs into the fort, dirty and breathless and shaken. They made their way up the stairs, down the hallway, up more stairs, and finally out one of the windows from the barracks level onto the top of the fort. They met the adults who looked them over, and then Frank asked, "Where's Allie?"

Chapter 6

The boys looked at each other and then back at their father. "Allie," John said questioningly. "She was here with you."

"No," said his father. "She ran out with you to go exploring."

"Well, Dad...," said John, speaking for his brothers without their argument, "we haven't seen her. We didn't know she followed us."

"No," added Jason finally, "If she was following us, we didn't know it."

By that time, Lacy was beginning to look panicked. "Well, if she wasn't with you, where is she?" interrupted their mother quickly.

The boys looked at each other. If she were just staying behind them in their shadows like a spy, she would be close; but each was thinking what no one wanted to say, and that was, "What if she was behind us when the roof of the tunnel caved in?"

Frank took charge. "She can't be too far away. Let's split up and go back in to search. Jarom and Jason, you check all the rooms on the top level and then come back here. Shout for her and listen for a response."

"Your mother and I will search the second level where we were last together about 45 minutes ago. Francois, would you go with John to search the lower level? The boys were down there, and you may know more places to look than John does." Francois nodded his assent.

"Shout, all of you. And then listen for her to respond. Check your watches. I want everyone to meet back here in 30 minutes to report on progress. And if you find her, come back immediately unless she is injured or something. If she can't be moved, then one of you stay with her and one come back to get help. Let's go!"

Allie had begun to follow the boys without them even knowing she was there. 'Allie, The Spy,' she pretended. The boys went down to the lower level talking about the fort, and she followed. As they looked around, she stayed in the shadows. She imagined jumping out here or springing out there to surprise her brothers. She would show them. And when they were frightened out of their wits, she would laugh…. But the time wasn't quite right for her big reveal, so she remained hidden in darkness, just outside of the light of their headlamps. And she followed.

Frank and Lacy hurried down the stairs to the second level and systematically began combing the hallways and each of the rooms. They both shouted repeatedly, calling, "Allie, Allie," to no avail. They came to the open area with the ruins of the old cannon foundation that had fallen down from above. Frank shone his light on all the twisted steel beams and broken concrete, but saw nothing. Lacy seemed to be in a controlled frenzy; with panic just beneath the surface. Her youngest child, her only daughter, lost in the dark, damp tunnels. "What kind of a mother am I to let her run loose down her," she recriminated.

Frank could see her tension and reached out to hold her hand for a moment. "We'll find her, sweetheart." They took a few more seconds to pray quietly together and then began again to search determinedly.

They searched the ruins of the old machine gun mechanism and, finding nothing, went back to the hallway and continued their tour, rushing from room to room; lighting up the corners with their lamps and calling her name; but finding nothing.

Jarom and Jason jumped down through the window and took off at a run. Their assigned level had more light on it than any of the rest and was mostly barracks rooms and, what appeared to be, offices. They ran through a latrine that consisted of holes in the floor that they peered down through. They called their sister's name repeatedly, but heard no response. Jason had the idea that she might have crawled out a different window opening and may have been on top looking for them, but it didn't seem too practical because she couldn't have climbed high enough to get through the window by herself. Then they came to one room with a window that had concrete blocks and rubble piled up high enough, so they crawled out on top, still calling her name. They circled around the top of the fort until they had returned to their original access without a sign of Allie. They jumped back through the window and ran out to the hallway, turning to search in the opposite direction this time.

John and Francois hurried down the flights of stairs to the lower level. It was darkest there, and John was a little worried that Francois might slow him down. He looked pretty old and didn't want him to have a heart attack or something, but Francois' health was good and his activity level was high. After a few minutes, John concentrated only on finding his sister. They toured the lowest level, running past the cesspit and the water tank, calling Allie's name. They listened but heard nothing. After they had been through all the barracks rooms, they came to the stairway that went down to the Travaux 17 tunnels. John looked down the stairs, and Francois asked, "Did you go down there?"

John nodded and said, "Yes, we followed the tunnel to a lookout tower and then came back."

Francois shook his head and said, "I should have told you to stay out of the Travaux 17 tunnels. They are unfinished and may be dangerous."

John said sheepishly, "Well, on our way back there were some rocks that fell from the ceiling of the tunnel, but we were past them......"

Francois said, "Come.....Let's go have a look!"

He started down the stairs and disappeared into the tunnel with John on his heels. John shouted for his sister but didn't hear any response. There was an echo, but only his own voice returned. They hurried down the drift and came to the place where Jason had bumped into the rotten support. The rocks had come down and blocked the tunnel almost completely.

John crawled to the top of the pile where the distance past the blockage should have been the narrowest and tried to dig past the debris with his hands. The loose dirt dug easily, and he soon had an opening that reached through to the other side. He took off his headlamp and shone it through the opening and thought he could see the continuation of the tunnel. He shouted into the hole and then listened for a response, but all he could hear was his own voice echoing back to him. After the echo died away, all that remained was the sound of his own breathing.

Francois asked, "What was beyond this?"

John answered, "The tunnel forked left and right. We went left and then came to a staircase that we took up to the top of a lookout tower."

Francois thought for a moment. The tower must have been added after the war because these tunnels weren't even started until 1917. Could you see what direction the tower was from the fort?"

John said, "Yes. It's in the woods, but we could see the fort from the top of the tower. I think I could find it from the outside."

Do you think she could be beyond this pile? If she were under it, I don't know if we could help. If she is beyond it, maybe we could get her out from the other side."

John looked thoughtful and then said, "There were trees growing up close to the tower. If I could climb one of the trees, I think I could get in."

Francois proposed, "Let's go back and meet with the others. Perhaps they have found her; and if they have not, then we can go and look for the tower." They turned and retraced their steps making for the top of the fort as quickly as they could.

Allie followed her brothers down the rough stairs into the tunnel that wasn't yet finished. She noticed that their lights were bright enough for her to follow, and they had no night-vision because of it, so they didn't even notice she was there. She would surprise them, for sure!

They walked along for several minutes, and then she heard them talking about the tunnel dividing to the right and left. She watched them go left and followed. When they came to the staircase, she stepped back around the corner. They ran up the flights of stairs, and she stayed back, one flight of stairs behind them. They started up the spiral staircase and, again, she stayed back around the corner. While they were up in the tower, she listened to them talk and thought about going up, but she wanted to scare them; not show up like a tag-a-long.

Finally, they started to come down, and she hurried down ahead of them. The stairs were lit from the daylight above. They were still talking about the tower and the stairs and radios, so she ran on ahead.

She finally had it! She would run back to where the tunnel forked and take a few steps beyond the turn toward the fort; then, when they were just about to turn, she would jump out at them!

She had her position: Crouching low in the tunnel beyond the turn she was ready to spring. She heard them coming by their regular footfalls, and she thought, "Wow, they're coming fast!"

And then they were there, had turned the corner running, and were gone. She hadn't even had time to jump out! She sighed to herself, "Well, I guess I'll just keep following them."

Dejectedly, she let them get ahead, switched on her own headlamp, and walked along the tunnel. Then, right in front of her, she heard a rumble. Suddenly, dust and dirt and whooshing air knocked her backwards off her feet. As she fell onto the ground the headlamp flew off and, smashing into the ground, went out. She was lying there in a tiny tunnel under an ancient French fort in the pitch black darkness. Alone.

All the groups met back on top. It had been just 30 minutes, but they all had done a reasonable job of canvassing the three levels. It was painfully obvious that Allie was missing, when John said, "We think we may know where she might be....."

They all looked at him and he continued, "When we were exploring down on the bottom level, there were stairs that went down further and we followed them into a tunnel. We thought it might have been one of the tunnels Francois said they had built after the war, so we thought we would explore it too. We followed it to a tower that we climbed up and, from the top of the tower, we could see all over. If she was following us and was trying to play the "Spy" like she does sometimes, we might not have known she was there."

"Well," Frank asked, "Why wouldn't she have just followed you back out?"

"On our way back, Jason bumped one of the wooden supports, and part of the ceiling fell in. Francois and I went back and checked it, and the whole tunnel is blocked off."

"Oh, Frank. What if she was buried in the tunnel?" cried Lacy."

"I don't think it was that big of a cave-in, Mom," said John. "I dug away at the top of the pile and I could see down the tunnel. I shouted through the hole, but she didn't answer back. It's crazy to think she would have even followed us down there and not let us know she was there, but if we've checked everywhere else. I just don't know where else she might be."

Francois interrupted, "John says that the tower is just down the hill. If he can show us where it is, we may be able to climb into the tower and then enter from the other side."

"Where's the tower, son?" Frank asked hurriedly.

John stood up and looked around from the top of the fort. Things looked a lot different from there, and he'd been trying to figure out the answer to that question ever since he'd emerged from the window. He finally pointed to what seemed like the east and said, "I think it's over there. It would have been on the other side of the moat, so we'd have to go down into the bottom and then climb up and circle around."

Frank made command decisions all the time, and this time was no exception. "John, you and Jarom go find that tower. Call up at the tower and see if you can get Allie to answer. If she doesn't, then find a way up into the tower, and go find your sister!"

Francois, if you can show me where the tunnel is, Jason and I will start to dig an opening big enough that we can get through. There were some broken pieces of steel bar laying around the foundation of that old cannon. We can stop there and get a couple of digging bars."

Francois nodded his agreement.

"Lacy, where do you want to go?"

She thought for only a moment and then said, "I'll go with the boys. They may need some help." Her unspoken message to him was that she really hated going into small tunnels, and she didn't think she would be of any help if she did.

Frank, Jason, and Francois started back down into the fort. They rolled in through the window, hurried down the stairs, and ran to the open area by the remains of the cannon where they found a short piece of angle-iron and another of rebar. Francois guided them to the stairs that led to the Travaux 17 tunnel, and they went in.

A few minutes later, they came to the collapsed ceiling, and Frank inspected the mound of dirt. He did not want to create a larger cave in, so he was reluctant to cause any movement. He examined the shoring nearest the collapsed ceiling and, unlike the post that had broken, the post there seemed sound. He crawled up to the top of the pile and, like John, could feel air movement.

He reasoned that the pile of dirt that was resting in the tunnel was, as of that moment, supporting the roof. If he could just dig a hole large enough to climb through, then he may be able to maintain the rest of the pile for support.

At the top of the pile, he started digging frantically with the angle iron, shoveling the dirt and rock back past himself, while Jason pulled the dirt down the mound with his hands and piled it at the sides of the tunnel. Francois was willing to help, but there just wasn't room for two diggers, so he watched and waited, expecting to give Frank a break as he needed it.

John, Jarom and their mother made their way down the broken cleft in the wall that they had climbed up earlier in the day. In the bottom of the moat, they walked around to where John thought the tower would be and began climbing up the other side. As they climbed, they noticed all the firing ports in the wall of the fort and could see how an attacker coming down the side of the moat that they were climbing would be under fire.

At that moment, however, the steepness of the moat wall was working against them. After they had climbed the 25 or so feet to the top, John took a moment to get oriented again. He led them through the thick woods in search of the block and stone tower that was at the edge of the hill in his memory.

They were about 200 yards from the fort but still hadn't found the tower. John suggested that they were as far away from the fort as he imagined they might have walked underground, and they were also approaching the edge of the woods where the view of the valley below would have given an observer the most panoramic of views.

They began to work their way around the fort, trying to maintain a constant distance; looking through the thick woods in the diminishing daylight for the tower. It may-as-well have been camouflaged because of its age and the unruly growth of the forest. Working around the fort clockwise, they had passed through one-o'clock and two-o'clock and now three. John thought that if they were going in the right direction, they would have seen the tower by then, so he reversed course and started back the other way. His mother and Jason understood what he was about and continued to follow him; peering up into the branches and striving to see through the trunks and vines and bushes.

Reaching their approximate starting point, they continued counter-clockwise and passed through 11-o'clock. At the 10:30 position, Jason noticed what appeared to be a stone pillar through the trees. He veered in that direction and, as he neared it, the pillar grew into a tower that extended up from the ground about 20 feet into the air.

They began to scream her name as loudly as they could, but there was no response. They looked up at the tower, and John began to wonder if he had been overly optimistic when he had thought that he could just clamber up a tree. Because of the density of the forest, each tree hadn't had much light in its development. The trees had grown straight and tall but not very big around.

John found a tree that was about 8 feet away from the tower that looked promising. He thought that if he could shinny up the tree and then throw his weight toward the tower, the tree would bend and drop him neatly onto the platform. He explained his plan and his mother, though she was reluctant to have John 30 feet in the air on a skinny tree trying to bend it over without breaking it, understood the urgency. With a silent prayer, she watched him begin to climb.

It was an advantage and a disadvantage that there weren't many limbs. Limbs make it easier to climb and to rest, but maneuvering around them forces a climber to change his climbing strategy as he spins around the trunk to avoid the limbs. Bending a tree in a particular direction favors not having branches so that there is nothing to counterbalance the climber's weight.

John reached the height he thought he would need to allow the bending trunk to deposit him on the tower platform. He held on tightly with his hands, put his feet on the thin trunk, and extended his rear end out toward the tower. He could feel the sway, but he just didn't have quite enough weight.

Tiring and in need of a moment's rest, he called out to Jarom: "Jarom! Climb up the tree and stay on the same side I'm on. When you get up here, we'll both lean out, and I think the tree will bend enough to set us onto the platform."

Jarom did as he was told, and, with their mother mutely holding her breath in silent support, he assumed a position right under John. At John's command, both boys swung their body weight toward the tower, and the tree began to bend. Then, just as if they had planned it that way, the tree deposited first, Jarom and then, John onto the platform. John tried to hold onto the tree so that they would have a pathway down, but the spring of straightening tree was too much for him, and it threatened to pull him over the edge of the platform. All he could do was let it go.

Allie sat up in the tunnel. It was black dark. She rolled over and got to her hands and knees to look for her headlamp. She felt around like a newly-blind girl; searching for the familiar shape of her lamp. Finally, her hand touched something smooth and round. It was one of the three batteries that powered the device. *Its fall to the ground from her head during her cave-in must have knocked open the battery compartment*, she thought, *and until she found all three of them….and the light, she would be in the dark.* Allie wasn't scared of the dark, exactly, but she was much more comfortable with it when she knew where a light switch was. She knew where the switch was, if she could find it and fix it, but she didn't have enough of the pieces to fit the puzzle together.

She continued to feel along the ground, and she came upon the elastic strap that had held the lamp to her head. She reeled it in, and the lamp was hers. Then, there was the matter of the other two batteries. She started a grid search, blindly pawing through 1 foot squares, but not finding her batteries. She was about to give up in despair when her roughening fingers felt something smooth. She picked up her second battery!

To help her concentrate, she closed her eyes in the eerie blackness and searched for 10 more minutes, groping only with her fingers. Her search didn't reveal the third, however, so she decided to change her tactics. She knew it wasn't very far back to the tower, and she knew that, as she got closer, the diffuse light would help her to see. She thought that if she could climb to the top of the tower, she could shout for help; or maybe even climb down. So again, like a blind person, she groped her way along the wall of tunnel, turning left when she lost the right wall, and, as she expected, the light improved every-so-gradually the closer she came to the staircase.

She began to climb the stairs when she heard, far down the tunnel, someone shouting her name. She ran back down the stairs into the dark tunnel again, shouting for all she was worth. She was afraid that she just didn't have the volume to make herself heard. Then, the shouting stopped, and she waited in the darkness to see if her own shouts were going to be acknowledged; but they were not.

Disappointedly, she turned and, with tears of fear and frustration running down her cheeks, she walked back to the tower and began climbing the stairs. Up, and up, and up she climbed; then she was at the spiral staircase. The light was much better there and, cheered, she trotted up the staircase to the platform at the top.

From the platform she saw the view that her brothers had seen only a short time before. She thought, *if all these trees weren't in the way, the view would be beautiful*. She could make out the mass of the fort several hundred yards away through the trees and could see through the edge of the forest to the valley below. Unfortunately, other than jumping the twenty feet to the ground, she didn't see how she would be able to get down. She imagined leaping out, grabbing a treetop, and swinging it to the ground, but she understood that what seemed practical in cartoons didn't always work out in real life.

She looked at her headlamp again. One battery missing, and the hinge that held the battery compartment closed was sprung. She didn't see how it was going to work again. To keep from feeling hopeless she thought of her mother and her dad and her brothers; then she began to cry in earnest because she *did* feel hopeless. She sat feeling lost and alone, but after a few minutes, logic began to once again assert itself in her mind; she took charge of her possibilities. She reasoned that there was no one there to help, that she couldn't get down, that her parents were probably frantic, and that the last time she had heard a familiar voice was after the cave in. She reasoned that, given enough time, her family would figure out where she was and would come for her. She decided that if she could hear a voice through the cave in, there must have been some way of communicating. Even if it was dark, going back to the cave-in seemed like it was her best chance for getting out.

She got to her feet and started back down the stairs. She noticed, as she left the spiral staircase, that the light was dimming. Soon, she was feeling her way along the tunnel again. She dragged her left hand along the wall as she walked; her right hand in front of her in case there was something she might run into. Of course there wasn't but, as a sighted person trying to be blind, she couldn't quite get over the feeling that she might, at any moment, smack her face against an obstacle.

She walked on for a while, and then for a while longer. After another while, she realized that there must be something wrong. Then, just as the tunnel made a sharp turn left, her right hand did exactly what it was supposed to. She was at the end of the tunnel and her right hand had kept her from smacking her face into the wall.

But there should have been no wall here. There hadn't been a wall here before, she thought.

In fact, she was quite sure she had walked much further than it should have taken to get to the turn. She was stopped cold with the sudden thought; *the turn!* She had been dragging her left hand along the wall and had completely missed the turn because the left wall was continuous. At that realization, she fell to the floor of the tunnel and broke down again. She cried to herself, *12 year old girls are not supposed to have things like this happen to them.* She pounded her hands on the floor, and the floor felt funny. She stopped crying and felt the floor. It was smooth.....and square.....and hard......and she got her fingers around the edge and lifted up. The steel cover plate came loose.

She mused, *It is pitch black at the end of a tunnel under an ancient fort in France and I find a box on the floor.* She moved the lid aside and reached down into the box. In the bottom, her hand closed on, what felt like, coins. The oddity was profound but, at that moment, she had more on her mind than a box and a few coins. Planning to have a look at them later, she put a handful into her left pants pockets and turned back the way from which she had come. She made a right turn and then began her trek back to the turn she had missed, dragging her left hand along the wall.

Frank had been digging with his make-shift tool for 20 minutes or so. His hands were scuffed with cuts, and his knuckles were bloody. He had made some progress but, as he dug, more dirt ran down into the opening. He didn't feel as if he was making much headway. At Francois' insistence, Frank slid out of the way to give him a turn.

Francois e began scraping the dirt away, as Frank had been, with the same disappointing results. Frank stood back for a moment to evaluate the problem more closely. Thinking like an engineer again, instead of an overwrought father, he asked Jason to make a stack of loaf-sized rocks. Then he left Jason and Francois for a few moments and climbed back up the stairs to the ruins of the cannon. He retrieved a flat plate of steel he had seen that was a little more than an 18 inch square. When he returned, he pushed the steel plate in at the top of the tunnel as Francois dug, and he braced it with the rocks that Jason had collected. The steel plate prevented the caving and, soon, they had started to shore up that part of the roof. The opening beyond grew larger, and they could feel the air moving through the opening. They shouted Allie's name; but to no avail.

Atop the tower, John and Jarom turned to descend the stairway when they found Allie's broken headlamp lying at the edge of the platform. Jarom yelled down to his mother, "Mom, here's Allie's headlamp. She was here!"

Lacy was overcome with relief! Feeling confirmation that they really were on Allie's trail, she shouted up at the boys, "Well, find her!"

The boys turned their headlamps on and started down the stairs at a run. They stopped at the bottom of the spiral staircase to shine their lamps around but, not seeing their sister, they began to descend the four flights of stairs down to the tunnel level.

As it had before, the tunnel grew darker the farther in they went. They hurried down the tunnel and, when they had come to the fork, they turned right. In a few minutes, they were at the cave-in. They could see the opening that Frank and Francois had dug and, speaking loudly, John said, "Dad, can you hear us?"

A moment later, Francois had moved out of the way and Frank's face appeared in the opening. He asked urgently, "Have you found her?"

John answered, "No, Dad. We found her head lamp in the tower, but she wasn't anywhere in the tunnel."

Frank, sounding even more panicked, said, "Then she must be under this debris! We have to move it!", and he started digging even more frantically.

Jarom had been worriedly considering exactly what his father had stated. He looked around his side of the cave-in when he saw, lying on the ground, a battery. He said, "Dad, I don't think so! She must have had the headlamp up in the tower after the cave-in. The lamp was broken and had only two batteries with it. Here is the one that was missing. It must have gotten broken here and then she made it back to the tower in the dark with only two of the batteries, because she couldn't find the third. The only other place she could be is down the other fork in the tunnel."

John looked at his brother and said, "Jarom, you are a deductive genius. You have to be right." And then to his father, "Dad, we're going to go down the other fork and get Allie. She has to be there, because there's nowhere else she could be."

They turned together and, with Jarom leading, headed back toward the fork. They turned to the right this time and alternately walked and called Allie's name. After a few moment's progress, they heard an answer.

It really had been a long walk. Allie didn't remember having walked so far down the tunnel, but she obviously had. She was tired and sore and disoriented from having felt her way along the rough floor and walls in complete darkness. When she heard a voice calling from far off, she imagined it was just her mind playing tricks on her. In a moment, though, the voice was louder and the word the voice repeated over and over was her own name. Relief flooded through her and she began to cry again as she shouted back, "I'm here! I'm here!"

It was only another moment before she saw the light of the headlamps through the curves of the tunnel and then she was holding on to her brothers with a seemingly everlasting grip. They returned her frantic hug and, after making sure that she was ok, started back the way they had come with Allie walking between them.

"How did you know where to come for me?" she asked.

Jarom replied like a big brother might, "When you weren't with Mom and Dad, we figured you must be trying to spy on us. It was just the process of elimination after that." Jarom sounded so confidant then but, along with the others, had been anything *but* only a few minutes before.

"I'm really glad you're OK, Allie," said John quietly.

"Me too," agreed Jarom. Then he added, "It's a shame Mom and Dad are going to kill you when we get back. What were you thinking, going off on your own in a place like this?"

"I wasn't on my own," she maintained. "I was with you guys. You just didn't know it."

Jarom decided to let it go at that. He knew that his parents would be so glad to see her healthy and well that they probably wouldn't even mention any of that.....at least not that day.

When they got back to the cave-in, Allie put her face up to the opening and Frank tearfully put his hand through the hole and cradled it.

"Oh, Allie," he said. "We've been so frightened. Thank goodness you're OK. Your mother is outside the fort now; all alone and probably frantic."

"John," he said, "Get back to that tower and let your mother know Allie is OK."

And then to Jarom, "Jarom, can you guys get down the outside of the tower?"

Jarom looked pensive, and said, "Not without some help. It's about 20 feet tall and we climbed up a tree and bent the tree over to get on the tower, but the tree swung back and we couldn't reach anything else from the top."

Frank said, "Well, this hole is big enough to talk through, but I don't think we'll be able to make it any larger without more shoring and some better tools, which we don't have, so I guess we had better concentrate on getting you down from the tower. You two go on back to the tower, and we'll come out and find you. Give us 15 minutes and then start shouting, so we can locate you outside."

At his father's instruction, John turned and hurried off down the tunnel. Running wasn't really practical because the tunnel walls and floor were so rough, but he made good time and was soon climbing up the spiral staircase to the platform at the top of the tower. He didn't see his mother right away, and he finally shouted for her when he noticed that she was sitting on the ground with her back up against the stone and concrete, her hands folded, and her head bowed. She looked up at his interruption and smiled because she already had an assurance that everything would work out OK.

John said, "Mom, we found Allie and she's OK. She was pretty scared, but she's OK. Dad said I should stay here with you. How are you doing?"

His mother smiled and said, "I'm OK. And I'm so grateful that Allie is too."

Jarom and Allie started walking back up the tunnel one more time. In a few minutes they came to the fork. *A left turn seemed so simple when there was a light guiding the way,* thought Allie. They continued walking and were soon at the stairs which they started to climb. At the top of the stairs, Allie looked out over the world again. She noticed that daylight was fading and then she looked down and saw her mother.

"Mom," Allie said, and Lacy looked up with tears in her eyes.

"Allie! I was so worried, but I knew you'd be OK," said Lacy, her voice choked with emotion. Then, she looked around and asked, "Now, how are you going to get down?"

The tree that they had used to climb up to the tower platform had sprung back to its original position and was out of reach. Keeping an eye on his watch, first Jarom and then, all of them began to call out to Frank, Francois, and Jason. They heard a shouted reply and then began to call out every minute or so, to keep the searchers oriented. In a few minutes, the troop appeared through the woods and, after giving Lacy a quick hug, Frank gazed up at the tower and asked, "Well, how did you get up there?"

John answered, "I climbed that tree, indicating the tall, skinny tree with a slight lean, and then Jarom climbed up behind me, and we leaned over toward the tower. The tree bent enough to drop us right here, but it sprung back and now we can't reach it," replied John.

Frank walked over to the tree and experimentally pushed on it. The leaves shook, but pushing from the base of the tree wasn't going to work. He thought a minute and then said, "Well, I'm clearly not as much a monkey as you two are, but I think I can probably shinny my way up the tree." And with that, he started scooting his way up. Because Frank was heavier and, because the tree had already been bent once, it leaned over easily enough. Frank swung his legs down onto the platform and then, continuing to hold on to the tree, he stood on the platform and said, "Jarom, slide down the trunk and don't fall! We don't need any more drama today."

Jarom grabbed hold of the trunk and swung his legs up high to get them around it. Then, he began to slide down. The further he went, the easier it was to slide because the trunk became more vertical. In a moment, he was on the ground.

"Help Allie grab high, John, and then lift her legs up so she can get them around the tree." John did as his father directed, and Allie was sliding along the trunk to the bottom of the tree with only a few scrapes on her arms to show for the whole day's ordeal.

John looked around one last time and then saw Allie's broken headlamp. He picked it up, along with the other batteries, and put them in his pocket. Then, it was his turn to slide to the ground. Finally, Frank threw his legs back over the trunk and, as he began to slide, the springy trunk uprighted, and he got a faster ride to the bottom than the children had.

On the ground, safe at last, the sun was gone and the woods were darkening. The van was still some distance away; on the opposite side of the fort from where they were standing. Francois began to lead the group back in the direction from which they had come. With a keen eye, he found his way through the woods to the van. They gratefully piled in, Frank started the engine, and they drove back to the campground.

Their arrival at the campground in the dark was again a disruptive one. The tents were collapsed, the bags were taken out of the tents and opened, and the air mattresses were flat. Frank looked at the scene in the car's headlights in disbelief.

Jarom shouted, "Dad.....It's that guy next door. He's trying to get at us for hitting his trailer with the football."

Trying to maintain a cooler head, Frank said, "Jarom, we don't have any evidence of that. If the damage isn't any worse than last time, it won't take but a few minutes to put it to rights. All of you: Please keep a civil tongue in your mouths and let's get this mess cleaned up so we can get some dinner and go to bed."

Francois seemed apologetic. "I am sorry, my friends, that you should be treated so badly here in France. Please allow me to help!"

Lacy turned to him, saying, "Francois, we understand there are bad apples everywhere. We don't hold this against your country. We're grateful we could come and visit, and we're especially grateful for your kindness. You have been a faultless host. Don't worry about the mess. The kids will have the tents set up again in a few moments. Why don't you just relax in your trailer? You must be exhausted with all that we have put you through."

He spoke again: "It has been my privilege. I hope our misadventure today has not put you off on exploring Verdun. There is more to experience, and I don't see how we can get in the kind of trouble we did today."

"Tomorrow?" she questioned. She had thought they had seen enough of forts and battles and was expecting they would leave the next day. Not knowing what to say, she looked at her husband.

Frank picked up the conversation then: "Francois, we don't want to impose on your hospitality. We are so very grateful...."

Francois interrupted, saying, "Pooh...It is nothing. I am grateful to you for allowing an old man like me to be a part of your vacation. Shall we say 9 AM?"

Frank looked at Lacy, from whom he was feeling a special tension, but he didn't want to insult their host. He said, "9 AM will be fine."

"Goodnight then," said Francois, as he stepped out of the van and crossed to his own trailer.

Because the kids were as quick as their mother's boast had predicted, they indeed had the tents set up in short order. Blowing up the air mattresses took a little more time but, while they were finishing that task, Lacy opened up the tote with the food in it. There wasn't much inside that was easy to prepare, and the hour was approaching 9 PM. She debated taking the time to fix a meal or giving everyone a granola bar and a piece of fruit and sending them to bed. Her day hadn't exactly been strenuous physically, but emotionally, she was worn out. Promising them a big breakfast, she passed out the snack foods, and no one complained. They discussed the day's adventures while they ate and, unlike the adults, they had expected to continue exploring the following day. With at least a dozen more forts, tunnels, barracks, ammunition bunkers, command posts, trenches, and miles of barbed wire strung through the forests, they felt like they had only scratched the surface. They were ready for bed but eager for more adventure.

Retiring to their tent, Lacy turned to Frank and said, "Frank, I thought we were leaving tomorrow."

He tried to console her, and said, "I know, sweetheart, but how could I be that unkind to Francois. I think he genuinely wants our company, and he's excited to show us around. We have plenty of time for EuroDisney. Let's give it another day!"

She didn't argue but, for the second night in a row, she slept so far away from him on the air mattress that he felt like he was alone in the bed.

Chapter 7

It was November of 1939. Winter had once again descended on the Meuse valley, and the town of Verdun felt the chill of the wind blowing in from the east. It wasn't only the wind that chilled the inhabitants of Verdun. Germany was rattling its sabers, and Verdun sat just over the border, directly in the path an invading army might take to reach Paris. France had valiantly tried, over the years, to fortify its borders and the overland approach from Germany, by building an every-increasing number of fortifications. The cost of building the new forts along the Maginot line was staggering, but that was in addition to the ring of forts that existed around the city of Verdun. Verdun's defenses had been built in the 19th century and modernized in the 20th, in prudent preparation for the periodic assaults that it had been the repeated recipient of since Attila the Hun invaded in 451 AD.

Then, with the likelihood of war coming, the French Army garrisons had been put on alert on August 21, readying themselves for attack. This meant that the forts and barracks and armories and books and turrets and shelters were staffed, and the guns were made ready to fire, supplies and ammunition were stored away, and training was accelerated to a fever pitch. The troops that were assigned to the forts around Verdun drilled and made ready for war, but the actual shooting war that would follow was still months away.

Germany had invaded Poland on September 1, and the border with Germany was immediately closed. On September 3rd, France declared war on Germany and tension at the front was at a fever pitch. The commander in each fort and emplacement was on high alert, the guards were armed, and the units were ready for an attack at any time.

Meanwhile, the soldiers had to eat, bathe, rest and take care of all of the mundane things in life when they were not on watch. It was the commander's duty to see that these things were done, so that the lives of the men would not be too stressful. Stress sharpens to a point, but quickly dulls its victim to uselessness. Of the many duties of the commander, one is to see that his men are paid. Even in wartime, paying the soldiers was important. There was often nothing to spend money on, but there was a boost in morale when the men had money in their pockets.

Capitaine Jacques Fontaine, commander at Fort de Choisel, had 290 men in his command. The sentries were patrolling the walk around the top of the fort. The High Command expected the Germans to come down through Belgium and knew that they might attack at any time. The Finance officer and his two guards had arrived in the afternoon and began to prepare the payroll for the company. They carried the cash to pay all the men in the division, and Fort de Choisel was their first stop. The Finance officer had been preparing to distribute the money to the men when the emergency order was received that put them on high alert. German attack was imminent.

The Finance officer was a bundle of nerves. He was usually in a safe office at the rear, and this was the first time in his life he had ever faced the possibility of enemy fire. He was trembling at the thought that he might be dead in a few minutes, and he could not function.

Because an assault was imminent, and the possibility existed that they would be overrun, and because the Finance officer was clearly not capable of carrying out his own duties, Capitaine Fontaine felt it was his responsibility to safeguard the payroll. He ordered the guards to join the contingent manning the entrance to the fort. He had the finance officer replace the money in the strongbox from which he had taken it; informing him that he would lock it away in a safe location, Capitaine Fontaine took the box away to secure it. There was no safe in the fort. He had an office in the "bombardment-proof" 2nd level but, in the event there was an intrusion into the fort, he wanted to secrete the payroll where it would not be found; there was too much money to risk.

In 1917, after the action in World War I, it was concluded that the forts could be better defended if a network of tunnels were built beneath the existing forts to allow access, escape, and resupply of food, water, ammunition, and arms to different locations in the fort and between the forts. The access would be safely and covertly done, without exposure to the battlefield on the surface.

The tunnel network had been started, and a tunnel existed from the 3rd level underground that ran to an observation tower outside the walls of the fort and also to the next fort across the valley, Fort du Chana. There was a separate network that connected various other strategic points within the fort itself. Because the tunnel network was incomplete and, because he was the commander and had inspected every inch of his domain, he knew of a cul-de-sac that had been the beginning of an access tunnel but had never been completed. He descended the stairs to the Travaux 17 system with his electric torch and quickly hid the strongbox in the dead end of the tunnel. He was certain that he was the only one that was aware the small room even existed and knew the strongbox would be safe there.

When he returned to his command, the men on guard duty were quite jumpy. More than once, they had demanded that intruders into their area of responsibility identify themselves; at gunpoint! When the Capitaine climbed to the surface and began to tour the perimeter of the fort, he was recognized. He attempted to calm his soldiers so that they would be alert; not hypersensitive.

Fort de Choisel was laid out seemingly backwards on the battlefield; a trapezoid with a point on top. Its point was aimed directly away from where the front lines were laid out. This was probably because its main purpose would be to repel an attack from the north, which flanked the main contact zone. Capitaine Fontaine had just come around to the point of the fort walking due south and turned at the point to the east. The picket that was assigned that sector was an unremarkable soldier and, when he saw the Capitaine arise from the dark as he had, he challenged him, pointing his loaded rifle at the Capitaine. Unfortunately, when he challenged him, he also inadvertently pulled the trigger on his rifle; the Capitaine was squarely in front of him. The bullet pierced his heart as neatly as if it had been aimed, and Capitaine Fontaine died on the spot. The shot from the rifle called attention to his sector, and suddenly there was massed firing into the woods in that direction. The imagined attackers, however, never materialized, and the only casualty was the commander.

As it turned out, the Germans did not enter Verdun until June 15, 1940, and most of the troops had been moved out in evacuation. During the rest of World War II, Verdun was a tourist destination for the German troops. After it was retaken in 1944 by the allies, it became a stronghold of the American troops or the duration of the war. The Finance Officer was held responsible for the lost payroll which was never found, and the soldiers of the fort in November, 1939, never did get paid.

Chapter 8

Morning came a bit later than it had the day before. Frank and Lacy were tired from their trial of the previous day, and the energy of the children was no less depleted. It was nearly 9 AM when they rolled out of their sleeping bags and began rooting around for food, and Lacy, followed by Frank, made an appearance a few minutes later. Lacy had promised a big breakfast, and she asked John to light the propane stove while she got food out of the ice chest. Eggs, bacon, pancakes and fruit were the solution to a slow-start morning, and she enlisted the aid of her kitchen crew to mix the pancake batter, slice the cantaloupe, set out the plates and silverware, and start the bacon cooking. Delegation was her strong suit, and preparations were well on the way when Francois crossed the street with a smile on his face.

"Good Morning," he said with obvious pleasure in his face. Despite the challenges they had faced, he seemed to be completely enjoying himself.

"It seems that you are still having breakfast," he observed. "I will return in a few minutes."

Ever the gracious hostess, Lacy insisted, "No Francois, please join us. We have plenty and we would enjoy your company!"

Though he attempted to demur for propriety's sake, he agreed and seated himself at the table. Apropos of nothing at all, he began to describe his own history and family. He related how, as a young man growing up close by, he had taken the spectral existence of the past wars for granted.

"Everyone here had parents and grandparents who had been affected by the conflicts, but life went on. We forgot why remembering our past was important. I went to University in Paris and eventually became a professor there, where I married and raised my family. After I married and we became parents of a boy and a girl, I taught history to others, but I seldom came home to appreciate the history of my native lands until those that knew the history were gone. I did not talk to my parents about what living through the 2nd World War was like, and it was different here in France than it was for your elders in America. Without America, we would never have prevailed, but America was never really threatened directly. Our country was taken away from us. We became actual prisoners of another power."

"I regret that my children did not learn to appreciate the more simple life that I had taken for granted growing up in this place, but living in the country was not exciting. The University was not here, and we were caught up in a faster, more glamorous, way of life. My wife was from Paris, and the village here bored her. She was unfamiliar with the people who lived here and their ways were different from hers. She felt unwelcome."

"My children grew older, and it seemed less important to visit. My parents died and there was nothing to come back for. I took a position at a University in America for 2 years and my family and I lived in Buffalo, New York. I taught at the State University of New York College. We traveled in America and glimpsed how large it is; how diverse it is; and ultimately how foreign it is. We came back to France; my children went to University and married, and now both live in Paris. My son is an Engineer and my daughter is a Graphic Artist. They are involved in their own lives."

"My wife died two years ago and I am older now. I retired and, as I think many people do as they age, I have begun to wonder about my own family history. I wanted to see where they had lived and how they had lived and what their experiences had been. I knew about the wars here, the facts and the figures, but I didn't know the people. I parked my camping trailer there the day before you arrived, with plans to put the facts and figures that I had learned in my profession on the ground, as you say. To feel how the war affected the people that have lived here by putting myself in the places they worked and guarded; the places they died in."

"I have you to thank for allowing me to experience these things with you. To see through your eyes and, through your reactions, what life might have been like for my great grandparents, their brothers and sisters, and their children. Some of them fought in these battles. I told you my Great Grandfather was General

Petain. He lived through the battles here as a general faced with the strategy of the war, the lives of his men, the attack, and the counter-attack. But he had a family; a wife and children, also my relatives. They lived through the horrors of the bombardment, the invasion, the death, and destruction of the war."

"And of course, that is the Great War; 100 years ago. The 2nd war was much nearer, and I have yet to try and understand my own parents' experiences. I will visit some of those places of battle as well. Now, I have been talking and making you listen for far too long. The breakfast is delicious and thank you very much. Anon, let me suggest what we may do today."

Jarom piped in, "Francois, you grew up here but you haven't visited since you left?"

"That is not completely accurate," he said. "France is not so large as the United States. I have traveled through the area and from time to time, did visit my parents who lived not far from here. But I did not play the tourist. I did not see Verdun from that point of view; or even from the perspective of one who suffered the trauma of the war. I just came home as a son to visit his parents."

John said, "So, Francois, you have seen these things before.....the forts and the monuments?"

"Yes," he replied. "But as a child, playing, sees them. As a playground, but not as a battlefield where so many died. As I said, because of my profession, I understood the facts and the numbers, but I hope to appreciate the sacrifice and the hardship as I put the facts in their physical places, if you understand?"

Allie, bored with all the introspection, said, "So where do we want to go today, Francois?"

He laughed, "After your adventure yesterday, you are sure you want to see more?"

"I love adventures. I want to have another one today. Where shall we go?" she asked excitedly.

"Lacy interrupted, "Francois, we don't really need an adventure today. A tour will be just fine."

"Well, I propose we visit the Tranchée des Baïonnettes. We have spoken a little about the importance of the trenches or, as they called it, trench warfare. Trench warfare sounds as if it was only a way to prevent an attacker from overrunning a position, but it was actually an evolving method of both offensive and defensive warfare."

Allie replied, "Is this going to be boring? It is beginning to sound like my brothers talking about football."

"No," said Francois, "I don't think you will find it boring. Of course, the trenches were built to protect an army's front line, but they had to be designed carefully to do that. In the same way, the design had to create opportunities to attack the enemy. Otherwise, it was just two armies facing each other; wearing each other down from a distance. Let us go to Fort Souville where we can see what the trenches looked like on the battlefield and then, to the Tranchée des Baïonnettes, where the restored remains of an actual trench exists."

They all got up from the table, began putting away the remains of breakfast, and securing the camp. Jarom muttered, "I wish I could catch whoever is trashing our camp."

Lacy suggested, "Maybe I should just stay here today. I'm sure they wouldn't bother it if I were here."

Frank replied, "Sweetheart, this is our vacation and we want you to be a part of it. It just wouldn't be the same without you, even if you are still nervous from our experience yesterday. I promise, this will be a day of safety. No danger. Right, Francois?"

"No risk at all. I'm sure!" avowed Francois.

"Well, there is one other thing that we have to do today, and maybe you can help us, Francois?" she asked.

"I'm sure I would be delighted," he said. "What is it?"

"I'm afraid that I am running low on groceries. I need to go to the store and buy a few things. Can you suggest where we might go?"

"Of Course! We are just outside the city of Verdun, and very near the Cathedrale de Verdun is the Monoprix where you may buy food. Do you want to go there first?" he asked.

"Perhaps that would be best," she replied thoughtfully. It seems that we have had a hard time getting back here before dark, and we're getting a late start today," she said.

Frank commanded, "OK, Family....Let's get in the van. First, we head for food; then for the trenches."

"And you too, please, Francois," he said more gently.

Francois once again took the shotgun position while the rest of the family resumed their accustomed spots. Frank started the van and they were off. Verdun city was a few miles to the south, and Francois suggested a route that would take them to the supermarket. Frank followed his directions and, in a few minutes, they stopped in front of the store and Lacy prepared to get out.

Frank asked, "Have you got enough money?"

She replied, "I got Euros before we left home. Don't worry."

"Can I come too, Mom?" entreated Allie.

"Sure, honey. You can help me pick out dinner for tonight," replied Lacy.

Francois said, "There are several things very close by that we could visit while you are inside, if that is all right?"

She replied, "Don't worry about us. We'll be about half-an-hour. Just come back and get us."

Francois turned to the group and said, "The Museum of Verdun is just across the river. There is a Great War monument almost across the street, and the Citadel is down the main road a short distance from here."

Frank said decisively, "Let's take a look at the monument. I don't want Lacy to miss the main sights, and we've already been to the Citadel."

"Oh," said Francois disappointedly. "You saw the subterranean tunnels at the Citadel?"

"Well, no," said Frank. We looked around a little and sat in the park for a while, but we didn't really see anything there."

"Well, the citadel was built hundreds of years ago, and much of it was destroyed in the war, but the tunnels are very much worth seeing. Perhaps when Lacy is back?"

"OK. Great," said Frank, and the boys agreed loudly.

"Oh, Boy!" said Jason. "More tunnels!"

Frank calmed his sons when he reminded him that their mother agreed to their extended tour with reluctance. He asked that they behave more sedately to keep from putting her apprehension in overdrive. They contritely agreed, and Frank said, "Well, let's see the monument, Francois."

Frank drove nearly across the street to the parking lot adjacent to the monument."

Sounding more and more like a tour guide, Francois said, "Here we have the Monument to the Victory at Verdun. It was started just after the war and finished in 1929. The sculptor was a soldier in the Battle of Verdun."

Jarom observed, looking at the figure of a soldier that was part of the monument, "That doesn't look like any of the soldiers that fought here."

Francois agreed, "No, this statue is of Charlemagne leaning on his broadsword. I suppose it is symbolic."

"Who was Charlemagne?" asked Jason.

Frank, who felt like he had to prove that he had a little knowledge of European history, spoke up; "He was a ruler of the Franks and became the first ruler of Western Europe since the collapse of the Roman Empire. When, Francois?" he asked, and then answering himself, said, "about 800 AD?"

"Yes, that is right", agreed Francois. He was also called Charles the Great or Charles I and, because he was French, we are still proud of him. Nevertheless, he conquered Western Europe and is the symbol on this monument for Victory in The Great War."

"Well, the real question," said Jarom, "is, 'Can we climb up the side of this thing or not?" And with that, he jumped as high as he could on the side of the base to see if he could get a handhold.

Frank began to reprimand him when it became obvious that the answer was "No" from an ability perspective and not from a permission perspective. Still, ever the father, he said, "Jarom....remember.....respect."

The boys contented themselves with running down the stairway at the front of the monument to the street level below and then running back up to the adults.

Back in the car, Frank checked his watch and said, "It's been about 15 minutes. I guess we should go back to the market and wait for Mom."

Francois pointed down the street in the opposite direction and said, "What if we drive down to the bridge over the River Meuse and see the Memorial of the Sons of Verdun; we will arrive at the Market in perfect time."

Frank followed Francois' directions, crossed the river bridge, and came to a large square where another of the many monuments of the Great War was displayed. They parked briefly and walked up to the statues. This time, Jarom was able to restrain himself, and he did not climb on the base supporting the statues of the 5 soldiers. Back in the van in only a few minutes, they arrived at the market just in time to pick up Lacy and Allie.

John jumped out of the van and opened up the back. He popped the top on the ice chest, took a bag of ice from his mother, and put it in the chest. Then, she organized the rest of the perishables and put the other groceries in the tote. Allie had already gotten back into her spot in the middle seat next to Jarom and, in a moment, Lacy stepped in and sat down next to her.

Jarom said, "Good news, Mom! We're going to see more tunnels today!"

Lacy started uncertainly, but Frank quickly added, "We're going back to the Citadel. Apparently we missed seeing the subterranean Citadel which has been made into a museum. Francois suggested we take it in since we're in the neighborhood."

Lacy smiled her approval, and Frank turned the van around and headed along the river toward the Citadel of Verdun.

Back in tour guide mode, Francois began, "The Citadel was actually begun in 1624. It was built on the site of an Abbey and was in the shape of a star. The star was a design used to increase the resistance to an attack. It had high walls but, in the 1880s and 90s, subterranean shafts were dug through the rock under the citadel to create an impenetrable fortress. These shafts now make up the museum."

They arrived just as François finished speaking, and Frank parked in the familiar parking area that they had arrived at only a few days before. They unloaded from the van and began walking to the entrance of the main tunnel they had missed when they had visited previously.

Francois continued his dissertation, "In 1914, the total length of the tunnels was 4 kilometers; by the end of the war they had added another 3 kilometers. The tunnels were used as the main headquarters and storage depot." Frank paid for their admission tickets, and they entered as Francois continued, indicating one of the displays. The sign on the display detailed the facts that there were 6 powder depots, 7 munitions depots, a bakery, a mill, a telephone and telegraph exchange that coordinated the communications for the whole Verdun defense area, water, kitchens, huge depots for storage, as well as shelter for 6,000 troops in the underground Citadel fortress.

Suitably impressed, they came to, what looked like, a Disneyland ride. They sat in moving chariots that proceeded along a train track to view the life-size dioramas of what it had been like to live and work in the Citadel during the war. They passed a room where flag draped coffins were displayed and from which the remains of one Unknown Soldier had been selected to be buried under the Arc de Triomphe, in Paris. On their way back out, Allie said, "That was interesting, but I like to see the real stuff; like the fort we were in. Is that where we're going now?"

Frank looked back at Lacy and said, "Honey, do you think maybe we should stop at a little café and have lunch before we head out to Fort Souville?"

Lacy replied, "That's a wonderful idea. I'd love a break from meal preparation, and we can all try some real French cooking! Do you know of a restaurant, François?"

"Not specifically," he said, "but there are many. Why don't we just walk down that avenue, and I am sure we will find one."

They did exactly that and, in 5 minutes or so, came to an outdoor café. They took seats at two tables and waited for a waiter to appear. One did, and with Francois' suggestions and translation, they selected their meals. Frank chose veal and pasta while Lacy adventurously ordered Frog Legs. Without completely understanding what they were ordering, the boys ordered escargots, fish soup, and sole. Allie wanted fish and chips and, while it wasn't England, the waiter did his best to make her happy. Francois ordered a plate of oysters.

There was such variety in their meals that they shared back and forth and ate their fill. The children were not terribly impressed, but the adults assumed the air of gourmands. Their meal finished, they were soon heading back toward the van for their trip to Fort Souville.

Chapter 9

The trip to Ft. Souville was short; in fact the whole battlefield of Verdun was relatively small and could be traversed quickly. In only a few minutes, they were parking at the visitor entrance to the fort. They exited the van and followed the footpath through the woods to the top of the fort where they saw the Pamart machine gun turrets. The Pamarts bore a resemblance to the cartoon that was drawn everywhere during World War 2-Kilroy Was Here. The cartoon was a representation of the outline of the top half of a bald head, an eye on either side, and a nose hanging down from off an edge that extended across the face. The Pamart had an armored top that resembled the bald head, a machine gun port on both sides where the eyes of the cartoon figure would have been, and a center steel projection protecting the area between the ports where Kilroy's nose would have stuck down. Lying on his belly and peering in the opening, Jarom announced, "There's still an old, rusty machine gun in there." Then, all the children had to have a look. Even Frank peered inside.

Francois said, "This is interesting, of course, and this Pamart is typical of those you might find on many of the forts, but the reason we came here was to see the trenches." He led them along one of the paths and then off through the woods to the east. The forest became more dense as they proceeded through it. Then, they were atop the edge of what seemed to be a hill looking across a valley below.

Francois continued, "We are standing on top of the edge of the fort now. Most of the fort that remains is far underground, but it received so much artillery in such a short time that the superstructure was mostly destroyed. The two Pamarts and the pop-up turret are about all you can see."

Pointing out through the woods, he said, "You can detect a depression that runs from north to south in front of us. If you could see out another 100 yards or so, you would see a second trench, and another 100 yards or so in front of that would be a third trench.

The closest one to us is the furthest from the battle front and is called the Reserve Trench. Next is the Support Trench, and next to the front is the Front-Line Trench. Beyond the Front-Line Trench was barbed-wire fencing in several layers, and the No Man's Land. Beyond the No-Man's-Land were the German trenches. Running from the rear to the front are Communications Trenches.

Dugouts and storage bunkers are dug from the wall of the trenches under the ground and reinforced. The trenches were approximately 8 feet deep with a step on the front to allow a soldier to fire over the top of the trench. There may have been duckboards in the bottom to walk on, because the bottom was often muddy, and the front, back, and top were reinforced with lumber or sandbags to protect the soldiers from gunfire and explosions. The reinforcement also helped to keep the trench from collapsing. The trenches were dug by hand and were not in a straight line, but zig-zagged. If the enemy penetrated into the trench, he could not fire down the length of the trench. Similarly, if a shell landed in the trench, the shock and projectiles from the explosion would not extend down the trench, limiting the damage."

Jason was obviously having trouble imagining the trench network.   "I don't get it," he said. "If there was a trench here, why wouldn't the army just go around?"

"Good question, Jason," said Francois. "There wasn't any around is the best answer, I guess. There was a trench network that ran all the way from the North Sea in Belgium, to Switzerland in the south. There were about 5,000 men per mile. Imagine the immense undertaking; to dig hundreds of miles of trenches by hand and then, to defend them."

Frank, showing he had learned a little history too, said, "The battle line wasn't always constant. The enemy would cross the No Man's Land and overrun a position of the trench and the defender would fall back to the next trench line. There, the defender would be reinforced, and then they would try to push the enemy back. Machine gunners were in sandbagged emplacements on top of the front line trenches firing at the enemy on the other side, and at anything that moved in No Man's Land. During the day, it was deadly to be in No Man's Land, but at night, patrols would penetrate under the cover of darkness to reconnoiter or invade."

Continuing the lesson, Francois said, "The Forts you have seen were part of this plan. They and the other artillery were set behind the trench network to fire on the enemy's trenches and guns, just as the enemy was situated to do the same from their side.

From within the trenches, soldiers could fire mortars at the enemy's location on the other side of the No Man's Land. Both sides developed trench mortars, which were like short range artillery that shot very vertically so that the shells would fall in the enemy's trenches. The mortars were small and mobile, so they could be aimed quickly and moved to another location easily."

Frank added, "There was no protection from the rain or the snow for soldiers that were on duty. When the fight was active in an area, the lack of sleep and the difficulty of attacking across the No Man's Land, being attacked through No Man's Land, the artillery barrages, the machine guns, and the cold and thirst and hunger were all terrible stresses. The constant sound of explosions, the collapse of the trench walls, digging new trenches or extending trenches, and the death and destruction on every side made the war so stressful that some men became "shell-shocked" or "battle fatigued". They lost contact with reality and couldn't function. Until recently, many of these men were branded cowards when, in reality, their minds were damaged."

Frank went on, "Then there was the mud that was always present. At some times of the year the rain is constant, and the trenches that ran through swampy land had to be completely sandbagged. Sometimes the trenches might flood and be half-full of water. These are all things that made this kind of battle so deadly. Each side faced the other for months, or years, just a few hundred yards apart. The commanders were constantly devising plans to most effectively attack the other side to defend against and repel attacks from the enemy. They didn't just sit and look at each other. They were actively trying to kill each other all the time."

"And that is why, as we discussed before, the Germans intended to 'Bleed France White' with their campaign at Verdun. Their General thought that his preparation and positon offered him such an overwhelming advantage that he would only lose 2 men for every 5 French. He was wrong, fortunately, but to the Generals, the life of each soldier seemed to be worth only very little," finished Francois.

They stood silently for a few minutes and imagined the war in full bloom from this vantage point. John, in particular, was struck by how the sheer magnitude of the effort and of the destruction could be related to an individual. "How very much like an anthill," he said quietly. "So many people rushing in so many directions, and no one cares how many die, just so they can keep the anthill running."

"Let's go down and walk in a trench in the woods," Francois said, as he started walking down the edge of the embankment. They followed, and soon they were walking along, what looked like, a footpath depressed two or three feet into the forest floor. Concrete posts stuck out of the ground on either side of the path.

"This shallow ditch would have been a trench 100 years ago. A century of leaves and grass and the normal life of a forest has filled it in so it is scarcely recognizable, if not for the posts that remain. The concrete posts were driven into the bottom of the trench and extended to the top on both sides, leaning away from each other. The posts were held apart by a wooden or steel frame, the whole assembly appearing like an upside-down A. If we dug down to the bottom, we might find the duckboards the soldiers walked on that were set on top of the cross of the A. Water in the trench sat beneath the duckboards. Behind the posts and against the sides of the trench were boards or branches that braced up the sides and kept them from caving in."

They followed the trench for a while and finally came out on a forest road. They looked around in surprise, recognizing where they were. They were in the spot they had driven to when they had first arrived and had been exploring in the van before they had gone to Camping Mairie. In front of them was the concrete archway, and the boys ran over to it. They noticed a much lower arch inside that had been filled in with earth, but through which an opening on the left side had been dug. Jarom slid in through the hole and discovered that the only light that entered was from the opening. Still, even with the limited illumination, he found he was in a room that had an exit into a tunnel. Jarom got a hand-up through the opening from his brother, John, and the boys returned to the rest of the group.

Francois said, "This is the Abri Caverne Infantry shelter and was the war-time entrance to Fort Souville. On the walls on both sides of the entrance are gun ports, which guarded the door. Inside, the second door also had gun ports on either side of it. As a young man, this was where my friends and I would sometimes play War!"

Jarom asked, "Have you been in through all the tunnels inside?"

Not for many years, "said Francois, "but as boys, we explored miles of tunnels that extended to the fort, as well as to the ammunition depot and storage areas 20 feet below the surface."

"When we first arrived in Verdun, we stumbled onto this entrance," said Frank. We were just exploring; we drove in from the road and just looked around. We thought about camping right here, but I was outvoted," Frank mentioned with a smile and a wink at his wife.

Francois said, "That probably would have been fine. From the looks of the tracks, few people ever come this way. It is just one of dozens, maybe hundreds, of entrances to the forts that have been abandoned and lost. Only the more adventurous battlefield explorers, like us, ever see them."

He turned as if he were going to lead the group into the tunnel, but suddenly scrambled up the side of the hill to the top of the concrete wall that formed the arched entrance. Standing 15 feet above the entrance, he said, "You can see the great depth of concrete and earth over the top of these tunnels and the rooms they lead to. There are levels below them, as well as vertical shafts for water. It would be a good place to come back to later with your headlamps.

If you can climb up here, we can walk through the woods and we will be back at the van in a few minutes, even though you can't see it through the forest from here. They followed him up the slope, and he turned and led them through the woods back to the van. He said, "I think you now understand the horror of the war. Let's go to the Tranchée des Baïonnettes. It is another war memorial, and I am afraid that you are getting tired of the war memorials, but it is the oldest. It commemorates the dangers of living and fighting in the trenches.

They once again climbed into the van, and Frank began following the directions from their tour guide to the memorial. They got out and walked to the massive stone entrance that led to a sidewalk on each side of an equally massive roof, 150 feet long, 10 feet wide, and supported by columns. Standing between the columns, they could see, what looked like, a hill under the roof. Steel spikes stuck vertically up out of the top of the hill.

Francois said, "This was a trench that a battalion was sitting in with their rifles pointing up in the air. A huge artillery projectile landed by the trench and the sides of the trench caved in burying them all. All that was left were the bayonets on the end of their rifles, sticking up out of the dirt. Whether these are the actual bayonets in the original locations, I don't know, but the story is a good one."

After the grisly story, they individually decided that they'd had enough of trenches for the day. Unasked, all began to wander back to the van. On the way back, Lacy saw a sign in French that she interpreted to mean, "Trenches that way." They had just come from the monument, and the sign was pointing in almost the opposite direction. There was a trail there and she asked the group, "I think there's another trench this way. Since we're here, shall we go and see it?"

Low grumbling quietly erupted from her children, but Francois and Frank smiled and nodded. Her request seemed so out of character that Frank imagined to himself that his wife was finally beginning to enjoy their vacation. He enthusiastically said, "Yeah, come on kids. How many times will you get to visit Verdun? Let's see what's here while we're here!"

With Lacy at the lead, they walked for a few minutes through the woods to a life-size display of a forward 'Fire' trench; No Man's Land visible just beyond. They walked along the back of the thirty-foot long trench segment, observing its 8 foot depth and the firing step in the front. The duckboards lay in the bottom and the revetment made of boards and branches that supported the sides.

Lacy actually was interested. She stood there imagining the terrible conditions that must have existed for the soldiers during the war. There were soldier manikins holding rifles and peering up through periscope viewers that allowed them to see the other side without having to put their heads up over the top and risk being killed from a lucky or well-aimed bullet. The sandbags were stacked 5 and 6 deep on the front of the trench and, in some places, all the way up the wall. Rusty barbed wire woven together formed a horizontal fence over the top of the trench that would deter attackers, as well as deflect mortar shells that might fall on the trench, bouncing them up into the air like a trampoline and, hopefully, away before they exploded. The trench was laid out in a zig-zag pattern, as they had expected, with a communications trench extending from the back to the front, demonstrating how men, supplies, ammunition, and communication would be distributed in the network.

As Lucy gazed intently at the depth of the trench from the sidewalk, she stumbled against the curb, fell forward against the wire railing, somersaulted neatly over it, and dove into the barbed wire canopy. Rusted as it was, the barbed wire broke and eased her to the bottom of the trench. She screamed in pain and surprise as Frank and the others looked on in stunned shock.

Frank yelled, "Lacy," and began running around the sidewalk from where he was. In a flash, he was over the railing and reaching down into the trench. Despite his frantic hurry, however, there was no easy way to extricate her from the sharp wire thorns that were tearing nearly every part of her body. The barbed wire had torn her clothing, and the barbs had ripped deep, bleeding gashes in her arms, legs, neck and face. Her trunk had been clothed, but the barbs punctured the clothing in so many places that she couldn't tell one piercing pain from another. The barbed wire still clung to the back of her blouse and she couldn't roll away from it without further tearing both the blouse and her skin.

By this time, one of the attendants, who was normally sitting quietly to the side, had appeared and was speaking loudly and rapidly in French. Frank couldn't understand a word he was saying and chose to ignore him in favor of helping his wife. Lacy was crying and trying to pull away from the restraining wire barbs. Holding onto the edge of the pit and reaching out as far as he could, Frank pulled the wire, whose spines were imbedded in her back, so it didn't spring with her as she moved. With another rip and a scream, she tore herself loose from it.

Frank wanted nothing more than to reach into the trench and comfort her, but she was at the bottom of an 8 foot hole. Try as he might, he couldn't reach her without falling in himself.

Francois, who understand the staccato bursts of French from the attendant, shouted down to Lacy. "Lacy, if you follow the trench around to the end, there is a maintenance ladder without wire over the surface that you can climb out on."

In acute pain with blood streaming from all her limbs, dripping off of her nose from the slash in her forehead, and soaking into her blouse from her lacerated neck, she was lightheaded and beginning to show the symptoms of shock. Though Frank was terrified at her condition, he was able to keep his wits about him as he climbed back over the rail and ran to where the attendant had indicated. He quickly climbed down the ladder and, in a moment, was around the corner where his wife lay weeping on the ground. He noticed the swelling on her forehead and realized that she had not only sustained a cut, but that her head had hit something on its way down. He began to worry that she might lose consciousness as well.

Not knowing the extent of her injuries and afraid to move her, he lifted her legs to the firing step to place them higher than her heart, and he began to examine each of her lacerations in turn. They were all bleeding, but none was pulsing blood. He tore off his own shirt and began to rip it into bandages that he could tie around her limbs to soak up the blood and help staunch the flow. The deep scratch on her neck looked ugly and could certainly have been much worse if a deep vessel had been torn, but the flow of blood was already slowing, and he placed direct pressure on it and on her forehead. He attempted to cradle her face in his arms and comfort her with his loving words.

Meanwhile, the children were beside themselves. John followed Frank down the ladder and began to help Frank manage her wounds. Each of them had received their share of injuries, but Lacy was always the caregiver; not the victim. Protecting her now was of paramount importance to everyone, and they both did all they could think of to ease her discomfort. Her cries had calmed to a regular sobbing as she said to her husband in a muted voice, "Oh Frank. I'm so sorry. I think I've ruined our vacation!"

Their vacation was the last thing on his mind. He was worried only for her well-being. Seeing his beloved wife in pain was far worse than suffering the pain himself and, other than trying to minimize the blood flow and comfort her, he was at a loss as to how to proceed.

Just then, they heard the unmistakable siren of a French ambulance announcing its imminent arrival to all. In a few minutes more, the medics were crawling down the ladder with a litter. When Lacy realized the fuss that she had caused she attempted to sit up, but she was dizzy and Frank insisted she lie still.

The medics, noting that there was no apparent life-threatening injury, began to assess her state of shock. One of them spoke halting English, and Frank was able to relate what had happened. He described her dive through the barbed wire which, though it made its own contribution to her injuries, did break her fall so that she only received a bruise on her forehead. Because she had hit her head, the medics would not chance moving her without stabilizing her neck in case she had a spinal injury. They finally strapped her to the litter, lifted her, and then carried her along the trench to the ladder.

In order to get her up the ladder and past the remaining barbed wire at the end of the trench, they had to position the litter vertically. With Frank below and Francois and the two medics above, they lifted her up through the opening and onto the wheeled stretcher. They quickly strapped the litter onto its wheeled base. Frank walked beside her; his hand resting on her arm. With the children and Francois following behind, they made their way to the parking lot.

Frank gave the van's keys to Francois who agreed to follow the ambulance. The medics loaded Lacy into it, and Frank climbed in beside her. Soon they were on their way to the hospital in Verdun.

The ambulance did not sound its siren, but drove quickly to the hospital and pulled to the emergency entrance. The driver opened the rear doors and the medics pulled out the stretcher and snapped the legs down. They rolled the stretcher through the doors beneath the sign that screamed in red, EMERGENCY. Frank walked at Lacy's side and, once they were in the Emergency Room, the Medics explained the injuries to the admitting nurse. Unhurried and nodding, she handed Frank a clipboard with a stack of forms to fill out. She began to wheel Lacy away to one of the screening rooms and was nonplussed when Frank accompanied her. In French, she told him that he would have to remain in the waiting area, but not understanding French he smiled and kept walking. Deciding that trying to argue with the big American was more trouble than it was worth, she allowed him to stay and went to get a doctor.

The doctor arrived a few minutes later and introduced himself as Dr. Albrech. He smiled warmly at them and then looked in Lacy's eyes and ears and at her forehead. In accented but understandable English, he told Lacy that they had to rule out a fracture. He said that, as yet she didn't appear to have a concussion, and that after they were sure her neck was OK, they would start cleaning up her other wounds. Lacy smiled at the doctor gratefully and then, with a few words to the nurse, he dispatched them to X-ray for a cervical spine series to rule out a neck fracture. The bleeding had nearly stopped, but the injuries were beginning to throb exquisitely, and Lacy gritted her teeth to bear it.

After a short elevator ride, they came to the X-Ray department which was fortunately unoccupied. The technician rolled her into a room and made several exposures; then disappeared into another room to develop them. Presently, he reappeared and handed the envelope of films to the orderly that had accompanied them, and they retraced their path to the Emergency Room. The doctor received the films and, after examining them, decided that there was no fracture. He unstrapped her head and arms from the gurney and then he began to more closely evaluate each of the lacerations and contusions.

"I have seen injuries like these before," said Dr. Albrech, "but I give you my congratulations. These are the most creative and extensive I can remember. I will have the nurse clean out each of the cuts and then I will return to place some sutures. How did you come to get so many?"

Embarrassed, Lacy said, "I tripped and fell into a barbed wire net over a World War I trench." I'm afraid I broke the wire.

The doctor replied, "I think you may have gotten the worst of it; the wire will likely not care. The nurse will be along in a moment. She will give you an injection that will ease the pain of cleaning out the wounds, and also a tetanus shot. I will return when she is done."

True to his word, a nurse appeared. She administered the injections and removed Frank's makeshift bandages which had been only moved aside for the initial examination. She painstakingly and painfully cleaned each of the lacerations and then helped Lacy remove her blouse to address the puncture wounds on her trunk. Then, because the blouse was shredded, she gave Lacy a hospital gown to wear and went to get the doctor.

Doctor Albrech arrived at last and began to sew up the worst of the injuries. Many of the barbs had scratched deeply enough to draw blood but not deep enough to suture. Wounds on her left arm and leg, as well as her the slash on her forehead, required sutures. He fastidiously placed each one and took extra especial care with her forehead to minimize the scar she would have after it healed.

After the ordeal, Frank helped Lacy back out to the waiting room where the rest of the family and Francois waited. He checked Lacy out of the hospital and received a bill for services. Fortunately, he had enough Euros to pay the bill. He wasn't sure what they would have done if he hadn't, but supposed they wouldn't have kept her as a hostage. He hoped that their medical insurance would sort it out when they got back home.

Frank tenderly helped Lacy into the back of the van and then started the engine to begin the drive back to the camp. "Francois," he said, "It seems that we are determined to ruin the exploration you wanted to do here. I suppose we will try and get a night's sleep and then head back to Germany so Lacy can get some rest."

Lacy immediately began to protest, "Frank, this is our vacation, and I can just relax for a day or two while you and the kids see the sights. We don't have to go home because I have a few minor cuts and bruises to heal up from."

He looked at her warily in the rear-view mirror and saw, in his mind's eye, a Frankenstein scar spoiling her beautiful forehead. "Honey, we had planned to go on to EuroDisney, but I can't imagine you limping around the park. I'm not sure what more we can see here that will interest the kids; they've already had a pretty heavy dose of World War I."

"If I can just lay on my air mattress and read for a couple of days, it will be the best vacation I've had in a long time. I'm sure you guys can find something *SAFE* to do around these dusty old forts. How many of them are there? 15? 20? In a few days, I'll be back on my feet and we can continue our journey. We have 2 weeks! I don't want to go back home and have you just go back to work. That's no vacation. We're staying here for now!"

Frank wasn't used to Lacy being quite so dictatorial and he suspected that it might be some of the medicine she'd been given that was doing the talking, but he thought that a night's rest would do them all good. In a few minutes they arrived at Camping Mairie. He pulled the van up to their campsite only to find that, once again, their camp had been trashed. Besides the tents having been collapsed, the vandal had pulled out the stakes and thrown everything that had been inside the tents around the campsite. It had not been raining, so the beds and sleeping bags were not wet, but the air mattresses were deflated and their bags had been turned inside out as if someone was looking for something.

Frank was grimly silent as he looked over the damage. "Francois," he said. "Thank you for all you have done for us today. I'm sure you are ready for a little peace and quiet as well." He stepped out of the van and asked the children to once again pitch the tents and organize the camp.

"I'm going down to talk to the manager." He said. "This is becoming ridiculous!"

He walked down to the office where they had checked in and rang the silver bell that was sitting on the counter. In a few seconds, a middle-aged man appeared and smiled at Frank. In heavily accented English, he said, "Ah….Campsite D-3. I hope you are enjoying your stay here!"

Frank said, "We have enjoyed Verdun very much, but three times someone has destroyed our camp! They have collapsed our tents and dumped out our bags. Have you seen anybody disturbing our belongings?"

The man was shocked. He said, "No. Never. We never have any problems. Are you sure it wasn't the wind; or perhaps a dog?"

"No," Insisted Frank. "This was definitely the work of a human. They let the air out of our air mattresses and turned our clothing bags inside out. I am at a loss to know why. When we arrived, the trailer in the next spot was parked partially in our area, and it was obvious that he had been using the space. I asked him to move and he did so unhappily. Other than that, we have had no contact with anyone else except the gentleman across the road from us, and I'm sure it wasn't him."

"Oh, monsieur, I am terribly sorry. I have no idea at all! Are you staying longer?"

"Yes, for a few more days. My wife was injured today and she needs a couple of days to recuperate. She will stay here at the camp tomorrow, but I am worried to leave her here alone if it would not be safe."

"Sir. I will personally watch your space myself. You can be assured that it will be protected. If she is resting, she will be undisturbed!"

Frank paused, and then finally said, "Thank you for your kind concern. I greatly appreciate it." They shook hands and Frank walked out of the office and back to the camp site.

By the time he got back, the kids had the tents re-erected and the air mattresses blown up. Lacy's sleeping bag was back on the air mattress, and Frank helped her from the van, where she had been resting, to the tent. He eased her down onto her unzipped sleeping bag and folded it over to cover her. He was concerned that as her skin and muscles stretched with movement, the air mattress would not be comfortable enough. On the other hand, he supposed that the pain medication the doctor had given her would also keep her somewhat sedated. It was about 8PM and, with the meds, she would be going to sleep for the night. He gently roused her and suggested that she make a bathroom trip so she could rest undisturbed. She groggily agreed, and he walked her to the bathroom and back and then eased her into the bed.

It wasn't late and the children were obviously still up, so he wandered over to their tent.

"Hi, guys," he said.

"Hi, Dad," was the joined response.

"What a crazy day! Other than having Mom do a swan dive into a barbed wire pit, are you having a good time?"

Jarom said excitedly, "Yeah, Dad. This is great! All the old forts and trenches and stuff really help you feel like life had been going on for a long time before we got here. The size of the buildings and the length of the trenches.....it is amazing that most of that work was all done by hand; no bulldozers or cranes or cement mixers. They must have had a lot of people working."

Frank smiled, thinking that maybe he wasn't the only engineer in the family, and said, "They did have a lot of people working. Today we use machines to help one man accomplish what dozens or even hundreds might have done not so long ago. On our vacation, we hope to visit some huge cathedrals that were built 1000 or so years ago. The architects and engineers and craftsmen that built those amazing buildings had far less to work with than those who built the forts here, and they constructed marvels that will be appreciated long after we are gone."

"Anyway," he continued, "What shall we do tomorrow?"

Jason said, "Jarom was the only one that got to go through the entrance at Fort Souville. I think we should go back there with the headlamps."

John agreed, "Yeah. That would make a fun day. Not really spelunking because they aren't really caves, but still it would be interesting to see where the tunnels go."

Allie chimed in, "I want to see more too! I just don't want to get left this time."

Jarom shot back, "If you remember, Allie, we didn't leave you....you didn't tell us you were there!"

With all the feedback received, Frank said thoughtfully, "I don't know if Francois has any desire to see more of the tunnels, but we can invite him, I guess. You know that if your mother was along, we wouldn't even be talking about it. But with her resting here, can I trust you guys to look out for each other and stay together and to be safe?"

They all chorused their assent and Frank said, "Who's up for a late snack, since we missed dinner?"

There started to be an enthusiastic refrain that Frank quieted with the reminder that their mother was sleeping. In a stealthier mode, they filed out of the tent to the ice chest and food tote where they encountered the goodies that Lacy and Allie had bought that morning. Normally, Lacy didn't buy many cookies or chips, but that evening they found a bonanza waiting for them. With plenty of vacation junk-food to fill their stomachs, they made quick work of the snacks and then went for a walk around the campground.

Jarom had his eye peeled for anyone that looked suspicious. He was determined to solve the 'Mystery of the Trashed Tents', but at that hour most of the guests were already inside and the brothers were the only ones who looked suspicious. They stopped at the bathroom facilities for a needed break and then walked back to their camp site. As they passed the trailer next to their tents, Jarom once again said with an accusatory tone, "I wonder if that guy isn't trying to get rid of us. Maybe he *really* wanted to put his lawn chairs on our spot?"

John replied, "Jarom, that's really crazy! We haven't even seen him since Jason bounced the football off his trailer," and they both looked at Jason. I really doubt that he would go out of his way to cause that kind of a problem. He probably just wants to be left alone."

They were just about to turn into their tent when the door of the trailer opened. To prove his point Jarom turned back to the trailer and addressed the man.

"Excuse me, Sir," he said.

The man looked up at him with a blank face.

Jarom continued, "Someone has wrecked our camp 3 times and we were wondering if you had seen anybody over there?"

The man again looked at Jarom, and then said with a French accent, "No. I have not seen anyone there."

Jarom went on, "Well, we'll be here a few more days. May I ask you to keep an eye on it?"

The man looked puzzled. "I'm sorry," he said. "My English is not too good."

Jarom tried again, "Please watch the camp?"

The man smiled, understanding. "Yes," he said. "I will help."

Jarom thanked him and went back to the tent where he reported, "The guy says he will watch the camp. Maybe he isn't so bad after all."

They all crawled into their bags and read for a few minutes before shutting off the lantern and going to sleep.

Chapter 10

Morning came too early for the whole James family. For Lacy, it might have been several hours later if the rest of the family had remained asleep. The children were, however, up and about preparing breakfast. Allie took the lead in showing her brothers that she could do all of the things that they could and, in the instance of preparing breakfast, they were willing to let her be their exemplar. She mixed pancake batter and lit the stove, heated the skillet, and soon had golden brown pancakes filling the serving plate. Butter, syrup and milk completed the breakfast meal, and by the time she had finished cooking enough for them, Frank had emerged from his tent too.

"How's Mom?" asked John.

"She hasn't done much more than groan this morning," said Frank. "I'm afraid she is going to be more sore than she expected. I wonder if we shouldn't just load everything up in the van and drive home. We could be there in 2 or 2 ½ hours, and she could recuperate in her own bed."

Jarom put in, "Dad, I'm thinking only of her when I say that her profound desire last night was for us to stay here and enjoy the vacation. I can't see how you could even entertain the thought of depriving her of her one wish."

Frank rolled his eyes and replied, "I'm so happy to see that altruism dripping out of your mouth, Jarom. Let me get that for you…." And he grabbed a paper towel that was moistened with pancake batter and rubbed it on the corner of his mouth. Soon, they were in a good-natured wrestling match with Jarom the very much underweight opponent.

Though they enjoyed the banter and the physical challenge, they were chagrined to hear Lacy say, "Frank, is everything OK?"

Frank turned Jarom loose and stuck his head in the tent. Its fine, Honey. Can I bring you a pancake? Allie fixed breakfast for us this morning."

She responded, "First, maybe you can escort me over to the rest room and feed me my medicine; then some pancakes would be nice."

Frank helped her on with her clothes and then led her over to the bathroom where she washed and brushed and combed to ready herself for the day. In the meantime, Allie had cooked 4 more pancakes and set them before her mother when she arrived. She took the pills that the doctor had prescribed and then began to eat. Each wound that a barbed tine had inflicted ached when she moved but, as she worked out the knots in her muscles, they hurt less. The pills began to take effect as well and when Frank could see ease on her face, he also relaxed.

"So what do you all have planned for today, "she asked?

They looked at each other before Jarom volunteered, "We thought we'd go back over to Fort Souville and look at some of the old artifacts."

"You mean go exploring through those tunnels?" corrected Lacy.

"Well, we might look around," admitted Jarom.

"Go ahead, but just remember these century-old tunnels can be dangerous, and I want to be the only one with injuries on this trip. I don't want to share all the sympathy and attention with anyone else," she joked. "Use your heads and be safe!"

Not believing how easily she had let them off, they replied with "OK, Mom" and "Thanks, Mom" and "We will, Mom."

Finally, breaking in to the discussion, Frank said, "I'll stay with them and we'll keep an eye on Allie. You know how girls can be!" He dodged a soft punch from his daughter.

"John, go see if Francois is ready to go, would you please?" he asked, and John stood and crossed the street to knock on the trailer door. He waited a moment and then knocked again with no answer. Finally, he came back to the camp and reported that Francois hadn't answered. They concluded that he must have something else going on, and they made ready to leave.

Allie gathered the pieces of her headlamp and Jason took it from her and began to tinker. He soon had it working again, but the battery compartment door was sprung and wouldn't stay closed, so he found their essential roll of duct tape and taped it shut. It performed nearly as good as new.

They took one last look around the campground for Francois and kissed their wife\mother goodbye after situating her in a comfortable lawn chair they had brought along from home. They made sure she had anything else she might need and told her they expected to return by early afternoon. A final check to make sure that their cell phones were charged and working, and they loaded into the van with Frank behind the wheel headed, once again, for Fort Souville.

The van covered the few miles rapidly, and they were soon turning off the main road onto the dirt track they had followed on their first day in Verdun. Frank pulled the van up into the clearing in front of the Abri Caverne entrance only to find a tent in the woods just off the track. Two men who looked to be in their early 20's were just getting their gear set for the day. They had spent the night there, just as Frank had wanted to.

As the James family exited the van, they turned and waved their hellos to the campers. Their experience told them that, in Europe, virtually any language might come out of the mouth of a stranger, and that sometimes made them reticent to be first to speak. The men saw the military license plates on the van and, like old friends from home, greeted them in English. The James introduced themselves as did their new acquaintances. Their names were Dan and Dan, which was confusing from the start, but the Dans were used to it and seemed to take misdirected references in stride.

Dan1 said, "We're from North Dakota, and we've been backpacking around Europe. We'd heard Verdun was a "must see" spot so we hitched here from Paris and found this trail up through the woods that led us to this great campsite. It looks like ghosts might live here!"

Speaking like a minor authority, Jarom began to offer them advice. "We've been here for a few days traveling with our French friend and we've seen a couple of the Forts the French built in their wars against the Germans. Where we're standing was in the middle of a huge battlefield! Thousands of artillery and mortar shells fell right here in these woods outside this fort."

The men were listening and looking interested, so Jarom continued, "You're camped right in a trench where men fought and were blown up in World War I. No wonder it looks like ghosts might live here. They probably do!"

Pointing to a rusted pig-tail barbed wire support that was sticking out of the ground next to a tree, he said, "Barbed wire ran through these loops and made a barricade right on the side of the trench you're camping in." The Dans looked at the depression their tent was set in and imagined that it might have been a ditch that ran along the front of the fort.

Jarom was getting into his role as tour guide now, and he said, "We could dig down a foot or two right here and might pull up any number of things from 100 years ago and with that he picked up a piece of pipe that was lying there and made ready to dig.

Just as he was arcing the pipe toward the ground, Frank stepped in and caught his arm in mid-swing. He relieved him of the pipe and said, "Jarom, let's have a look at that pipe you're about to bash into the ground." He turned it over and started to pick away at the other end that was plugged with mud and rust. In a moment, a round shape began to appear in the midst of the mud, and, when he had freed it sufficiently, he was able to work it out. The object had a peculiar bomb-like appearance, and Frank gingerly laid it on the ground and said, "This is called a mortar, Jarom, and that is a mortar shell. Normally the pipe is placed on the ground and the shell is dropped down the pipe. A pin in the bottom causes the first stage of the mortar to fire and it shoots out of the tube and falls where you aimed it and, hopefully, it waits to explode until it's there."

Frank continued, "Old shells like this have been laying in the mud for a century and the time and the rust have inactivated most of them. Still, the French and the Belgians have government agencies whose employees spend every day collecting the old unexploded ordinance that is found by farmers and hikers, and they detonate it in a safe location." He related to the newcomers what had happened to them the day they had arrived at the construction site and the men were somewhat nonplussed.

"Anyway," Frank volunteered, "we were about to have a look at some of the passages in this old fort if you want to come along."

The Dans looked at each other and graciously demurred. Dan2 said, "You guys go ahead. We'll poke along at our own speed. We don't want to hold you up."

The James said goodbye and walked over to the entrance to have a look. Jarom had already been through the arch, and then he had crawled through the opening that had been cleared by earlier explorers, but the others had not. They had to belly-crawl through the small opening, and when they were all inside and had switched their headlamps on, they looked at the room they were standing in. There were hallways extending past the entrance on both sides that soldiers could stand in and control access by shooting though firing ports that covered the entrance. They turned and, with John and Jason at the lead, began to walk down the tunnel. It darkened quickly as they got further and further away from the entrance. They were grateful for their headlamps, as they could see how dangerous walking through the tunnels and rooms might be without them.

The ceiling of the tunnel, really a room 20 feet wide, was arched from side to side. They passed through the room into a narrower passageway that descended gradually to the level below. They noticed that on the lower level, the red line indicating a fortified ceiling appeared at the upper edges of the wall. The passage forked left and right. John had thought about this moment for a day now, and he pulled out of his pocket a large piece of chalk. He turned to the wall and drew an arrow on the wall indicating the way out, and the others congratulated him on his foresight.

They took the left passage which quickly broadened into a wide room with a tall arched roof that looked like the inside of a large Quonset hut. Frank speculated that it might have been a cave shelter. He said that there were several in Fort Souville and that they stored supplies and ammunition as well as housing hundreds of people in them. Bricks had fallen from the walls and the wooden ceiling was gone, but its size was impressive. They continued through it to the other end and came to a gallery leaving the shelter with a rail track running through it. The floor of the gallery was confusing because it was uneven; not flat but undulating higher here and lower there, as if piles of dirt had been left about covering the track. The ceiling was intact, and there was no obvious source for all the dirt. Then, they came to an unfinished tunnel branching off to the left that appeared to be a Travaux 17, and John said, "They dug this after the war....I wonder if they were dumping the dirt that came from the Travaux 17 tunnels in the other passage; intending to remove it later. Then, when the project was abandoned, the dirt was never hauled away?" That seemed reasonable, and the rest nodded in agreement.

Following the tracks, they came to what must have been a kitchen. There was a chimney and, what looked like, the remains of ovens built into the wall. The room was spacious, and broken brick and stone counters were convenient to the ovens.

It was completely black without the headlamps and, while the others were imagining the kitchen in operation, Jarom took a step through a narrow opening into the next room. It was nearly one step too many. The floor went out from beneath him, and he found himself sitting on the edge of a vertical shaft that measured 6 feet square with iron rungs that descended into the blackness below. He sat for a moment; his heart pounding at the big step he'd almost taken and slid back away from the hole.

In different circumstances, he had become quite used to climbing up and down similar shafts. In this instance however, the surprise rattled him and, with his hands trembling but still not sharing the plunge he had nearly made, he turned and called everyone's attention to the room with the shaft. They all stuck their heads in to see it and began to speculate as to its purpose.

Jason said, "Maybe it was the toilet."

"Or maybe a shaft for a missile launcher," Jarom joked.

John opined, "Or a well?"

Jarom proposed, "Well how about if I climb down and see what's at the bottom," he said, rolling his eyes toward the quarter he feared rejection from.

Frank looked pensive for a moment, and then said, "I suppose that isn't much different than the shafts near our home. "(Note from the author: If you don't understand this reference, you really need to read 'The Closet') "Do you think you can climb down those rungs safely, Jarom?"

"Sure Dad"

"Do you want to go with him and keep him out of trouble, John?"

Not expecting this line of tolerance, John stammered, "Uhhh, yeah."

"OK", said Frank. "We'll be right here with our lights pointed down. If there is anything wrong with the ladder or any other problem, I want you right back up here."

Without another word, Jarom edged around the shaft. Sitting with his knees over the ladder rungs and his legs extending down into the hole, he swung around to get a foothold on a rung and started to descend. John repeated the actions and, in a few seconds, both boys were on their way down. They felt a constant breeze rising through the shaft as they descended and, while they were still visible to the watchers above, they came to a horizontal shaft on their left that opened into blackness. Not wanting to step out of sight of the watchers at the top of the shaft, Jarom continued on toward the bottom. They climbed on and on, the size of the opening at the top becoming smaller. Finally, Jarom touched the bottom. Before letting go of the rungs, he swung the light around to make sure there was stable footing and then he let go of the ladder and gingerly stepped on the damp ground. There was the smell of wet gravel, and he was noticing some debris covering the bottom when John stepped down beside him.

There really wasn't much room to move, and junk had apparently been tossed into the hole. There were bricks and rocks strewn about. Pieces of lumber, lengths with one end resting on the ground and the other tipped up against the wall and others piled haphazardly around the space, were crowding them in. There was barely enough gravel for both of them to stand.

John squatted and looked at the debris more closely. He noticed small skeletons that had been there for quite a while. He thought that they were likely rats or mice that had fallen into the shaft and had decomposed over time. The moisture there would have contributed to their gradual decay and there was no smell, so their demise wasn't recent.

Meanwhile, Jarom began rummaging around under the boards. He tipped them out of the way and made a similar, but far more startling, discovery. Under the boards, he found a human skeleton; broken and disarticulated, but obviously there. There were clothing remnants, but the moist surroundings had encouraged bacterial growth that had left them in tatters. Decomposition had left a partially disarticulated skeleton from the human body that must have once fallen down the shaft. John turned to look at what Jarom had discovered and found a chain around one wrist-bone that had a silver disk on it. The disk read 317 and AUXERRE, a sort of perforation, and it read the same thing again.

The boys had been raised in the age of CSI and, beyond visual examination, didn't touch anything else. They wondered aloud about the bracelet and the tag, the age of the remains, and what they should do.

By that time their family members at the top were becoming impatient. Jason yelled, "Are you guys alright?" the sound echoing off the sides of the shaft.

John yelled back, "Yeah, we're fine. We found a skeleton!"

At that distance through the shaft, John's reply was not completely intelligible. They heard more shouting from above but, having seen the contents of the shaft and not understanding what was being said, they began to climb back toward the surface.

10 minutes later, as they stepped back into the tunnel and away from the vertical drop, they excitedly began to relate what they had found. Jarom said, "I found a human skeleton down there!

A lot of junk had fallen in on top of it, and when I moved the stuff off, the bones were lying there.

Frank asked concernedly, "Was there any identification on the body?"

Jarom quickly answered, "John found a chain around the wrist with an identity tag on it....sort of like the dog tags you wear, Dad. It said, "317 AUXERRE."

Frank mused, "You're probably right. Maybe that is what the French wore for dog tags in World War I. It's strange that the remains hadn't been found before. You two certainly can't have been the only explorers in the last century."

John said, "Well, the bones were completely hidden. Unless someone was curious enough to move a whole pile of broken boards off the top of him, I don't think they would have found him. It's clear that he's been there a long time, though. There was almost nothing left of his clothes, or skin, or even hair."

Allie said, "You guys are just gross! Some poor man is down there, and you talk about him like he is part of the trash-pile."

"We'll have to report him to the authorities when we get back, but I suppose he has been there long enough that it won't matter if we wait a few hours," said Frank.

"Anyway," continued John, "on the way down, there is another tunnel that goes off to the side. We didn't go into it yet, but we felt a lot of air coming out of the tunnel and going up the shaft. Can we go look?"

"Can all of us get safely off the ladder and into the tunnel, "asked Frank?"

"Easy!" replied Jarom with confidence.

"Then why don't we all go and see where it leads," proposed Frank. He continued, "I've been thinking about the possible purposes for a vertical shaft like this. It could be a well that was filled in or that had gone dry. After all, there's no water down there now.

It could be an air shaft to circulate fresh air through the rest of the tunnel system and to the fort, and the airflow you've all felt make that very likely. My last thought is that it might be an escape exit. The French may have mined the entrance we came through so that if it were overrun, they could blow it up to keep the invaders out. To escape, a shaft like this one would have let them go to another level that might have led to an exit. This shaft may do exactly that; it may lead to an exit. Jarom, you take the lead again, and Allie, you follow right behind him."

Frank followed Allie, with Jason and then John bringing up the rear. As they stepped off the ladder and into the dark tunnel, because of the closeness of the walls, it appeared even darker than it had before. Keeping the same order that they had descended the ladder in, they started through the drift. They followed the tunnel straight for a distance and then turned to the left when it branched left and right. They took the right fork at the next bifurcation. They had thought it would be easy to follow the airflow but, as they walked along, the air became still and more stagnant. They concluded that they had missed the air supply tunnel.

After his last misstep, Jarom kept his eyes out for another vertical drop but didn't find one. He took a right at the 4-way intersection he came to next and then, splitting left at the following turn, they finally came to a blind end. They came about, and John turned to lead. He reversed their course and turned on to, what seemed, a bigger passageway to the left at the next opportunity. He continued along that one and discovered more large rooms with high curved ceilings to the right and left. They walked through two of the rooms, grateful to be in a larger space for a while but, at the opposite end, found themselves again in a smaller tunnel.

They had burned up an hour with wandering around. Not finding anything significant, Frank pointed out that maybe they should begin heading for the exit. It was only then that, if they could have seen his face more clearly, they might have noticed that it had turned a chalky white.

He stammered, "I forgot to mark the walls with the chalk! I don't know where we are."

They all looked at him. Everyone was dead silent. Recriminations were not useful so no one castigated him, but he berated himself saying, "I can't believe I was so stupid!" He paused for a moment and then said, "We haven't turned that many times. We should be able to just retrace our steps."

With general agreement, they began to do what they thought was just that. Suddenly, the tunnel they were walking in ended. They all turned to look at each other.

Frank said, "There are miles of tunnels in this fort alone, let alone those that may communicate with another fort or bunker or arsenal. We don't want to be lost and going around in circles. John, starting now, mark both sides of every each tunnel we are in when we enter it or when we leave it at another intersection. Then, we will know we've been there before. With that he took the lead, trying in vain to imagine where they might be. He walked along choosing one way or the other at various splits, and John faithfully marked the tunnels as they had agreed.

Frank's logic was to try and identify which of the passages was the larger and to take it. He reasoned that a bigger tunnel meant more traffic, and more traffic would lead them to an exit sooner or later. He came to a 4-way intersection and saw one of the other openings had John's chalk marks. They were glad that they had been protected from wandering in circles, and he turned into a different tunnel.

They began to feel air moving on their faces again. Frank checked his watch ; he had been leading the expedition for an hour. Still, he had no confirmation that they were any closer to an exit than when he had begun. He could not imagine the purpose of this warren of small tunnels when he finally noticed four three-foot high openings on the side of the tunnel. He stuck his head in the first and saw a round hole about 10 inches in diameter in the roof of the tiny chamber that measured about 3 feet square. He moved to the next and saw the same thing, and the same in the third and fourth.

Feeling a little better, he turned to his followers and said, "And what do you suppose these were for?"

They were unsure, but he said, "Imagine what these might look like from the above." And then they had it. They were standing in the service gallery beneath latrines. They must have had a container that they slid into the openings to catch the waste dropping through the holes. With exclamations of both disgust and relief, they realized that there must be a way to get to the other side of the toilet seats and, in a few minutes, they had found it.

From the top, they actually may not have recognized what they were looking at. It just appeared as a pile of rubble with fairly inconspicuous holes in the floor. But if there were 4 latrines, then it must have been a populated place at one time. Just a little further along, they couldn't see an exit, but there was a gun port with light coming in. They were close to getting out!

Finally, they came to stairs. Jason and Jarom ran up the stairs and discovered the turret platform for one of the big guns. While they were looking at the hand-crank elevator that hoisted the ammunition up to the gun level, Frank was examining big pipes bolted together and running to and from what he thought must have been a boiler. He decided that the huge turret above them which had a massive iron dome was raised and lowered by steam power from the boiler. John had climbed down through the supports for the huge turret into the pit below to see it from that angle. After crawling all over the mechanism and feeling much more at ease with the world in partial daylight, they once again began to look for the exit from the fort. Though it was partially buried in debris, they found their way out into the open.

Now the problem was getting back to the van. Standing on top of the steel turret, they looked at the terrain and finally decided that they were not far from where the family had stood with Francois just the day before. They started down the slope and soon found themselves in the remains of the old trench and, before long, were walking into the clearing where the van was parked.

Chapter 11

Coming back to their morning starting point, they were surprised to find the Dans still there. They had been busy digging in the trench beside their tent. In the absence of the James family, they had unearthed all manner of treasures from the trench. It had taken them a while to locate digging implements, but searching around through the woods led them to a flat sheet of stiff metal that they had used as a shovel. A complete barbed wire support served as a digging bar.

Their unauthorized archeological dig had yielded some sobering finds. To begin with, they had uncovered a growing pile of bone fragments. It was as if this had been a depository for random body parts found on the battlefield. There seemed to be no consistency as to the parts that they had uncovered. Two left legs and a right arm, and so on. Given their location at the front of a fiercely fought and heavily defended battlefield, it may have been an impromptu burial site. That would be one more thing they would relate to the authorities on their return, thought Frank.

Speaking to the Dans, Frank said, "Hey, guys, I'm not sure about the legality of your digging, but I expect that the human remains that you've found are protected under French law. Maybe you should consider stopping your excavation so that it can be done properly by the experts."

Dan1 looked up and said, "Oh. We never thought of that. Jarom gave us the idea this morning, and he was right! There is so much stuff buried all over out here!"

Dan2 started to give them a tour of what they had found. "Look at all these shell fragments," he said, showing them a pile of shrapnel that he had added to, piece by piece, as he had uncovered them in his hole. There were also many rusted pieces of barbed wire, both long and short as well as other random but unidentifiable objects.

He picked up what appeared to be a rusty pipe four feet long. He began to pick away at one end of the pipe and, as the dirt fell away, he discovered a trigger guard and the rusted bolt of a long-forgotten rifle that had been abandoned in the trench.

There were even some artifacts that the James were already familiar with. For instance, there was a pile of rusted cans, some with a stick-like handle on one end. They quickly recognized them as hand grenades and were somewhat nervous to see them being moved about. There were mortar shells that had not been fired, and another shell that was larger and also appeared unfired.

Frank said, "Dan, you know that this is unexploded ordinance from World War I."

Dan2 replied, "Yeah. It's amazing. After 100 years, it's all still here. I read about old ammunition like this a while back," he said. "The article said that after so many years, the shells have rusted and water that has leaked inside the shells ruins the gunpowder so they are no longer explosive. I'm not too worried about them." He turned to what he obviously regarded as his most prized find and, holding it up, he said, "And look at the shape this beauty is in! It looks perfect."

It did look pristine. There was rust on the body and it was painted a dull yellow, but compared to the other projectiles, it was in very good shape. Then Frank noticed that the shell was leaking! A gentle stream had poured out of the middle of the rusted area and had run down into Dan2's shirt sleeve and then into the leg of his pants.

Suddenly he threw the shell to the ground and yelled, "Something is burning me!" and he started beating the leg of his pants with his hands. His hands reddened and began to burn wherever the wet stain on his pants had touched his hands. Then, he began tearing at his shirt sleeve in an attempt to get it off of his arm.

Frank knew instantly what had happened. World War I had been the dawn of chemical weapons and they were used extensively. Tear gas had been used successfully, first by the French and then by the Germans. The Germans began experimenting with Chlorine gas and then Phosgene gas, and they were soon copied by the allies. The gas was first used by releasing it from tanks, and then depending on the wind to carry it to the enemy. The variability of the wind made the delivery so uncertain that they devised a method of releasing it from artillery shells but, even under good conditions, gases were often ineffective. The gases were heavier than air and so dependent on the weather and wind conditions that they often harmed the attacker more than the intended recipient.

The Germans soon began producing the most effective of the World War I chemical weapons; Mustard Gas. Mustard Gas was a persistent chemical that initially caused blisters on exposure to the skin and destroyed the lining of the lungs when inhaled. Because it degraded slowly, it could make terrain difficult to cross without contaminating one's own troops. The Allies quickly made their own version of Mustard Gas and, by the end of the war, the horrors of chemical warfare were so terrible that the weapons were outlawed by the Geneva Convention in 1925. In World War I there were about 1.3 million chemical weapon casualties, and Frank was witnessing the latest one before his very eyes. He knew that the Germans color-coded their gas shells, and the Mustard Gas shells were yellow.

Frank became the efficient commander in charge, and said, "You've been exposed to a chemical agent from that shell. Don't touch your hands to any other body part! We've got to get those clothes off of you to limit your exposure."

"What does it do?" asked Dan2 starting to panic.

Dan1 had come over and could see where his buddy's hands were becoming red.

Frank continued, "See how this shell is painted yellow? The Germans used yellow to indicate a shell containing mustard gas. If the shell had exploded, it would have dispersed the contents over a broad area, and we would have had an aerosol to deal with as well. Instead, the shell leaked and you've got the concentrated liquid running down your arm and leg. To reduce the exposure we need to get those clothes off of you, and we can't contaminate ourselves in the process."

He pulled out his pocket knife which he kept sharpened to a razor-edge. Starting at the sleeve cuff on the opposite side of the wet stain, he began to slit the fabric up to Dan2's armpit, and from there cut all the way around the shoulder. Then, taking care not to touch or smear the liquid further on Dan's arm, he rolled the sleeve down his arm away from his body. Where the liquid had touched the skin, the arm was bright red.

Frank set the contaminated sleeve aside and began the same process with the leg of his pants. By the time the pant-leg had been removed and the reddening leg was exposed, only a few minutes had passed. If they could find enough water they could dilute the substance on Dan's skin to minimize the tissue damage that was taking place. They emptied their water bottles over his leg and arm, but they didn't have enough water to sufficiently dilute the exposure, so they all got into the van and Frank drove to the Verdun Memorial they had visited at Fleury which was only a few minutes away.

They emerged from the van and hurried up the steps and into the building. Dan2's appearance was not that of the typical tourist. With one arm and one leg completely bare, the attendant inside surmised that something was amiss. Communicating with sign language and English, they made themselves understood well enough to be directed to the rest room. There were two sinks set into the counter and, with his leg under one faucet and his arm under the other, they flushed a stream of water over the contaminated areas for several minutes.

Finally, having done all that they could, and with Dan's arm and leg still reddening but no longer harboring contamination dangerous to others, they dried his limbs with paper towels and walked out of the rest room door. A small managerial crowd had gathered outside the door and Frank did his best to relate what had happened, but he was unsure he had been successful. Nevertheless, they thanked the concerned staff and left the building.

Dan2 asked, "Now what am I supposed to do? My clothes are ruined and my hands and arm and leg still burn."

Frank replied, "After exposure, blisters will begin to form within a few hours. It depends on the extent of the tissue damage from the chemical, and we got it washed off pretty quickly. I suppose the best plan would be to get you to the hospital to let them check you out. My guess is that this won't be the first case they've seen like yours and they will know what to do.

Since the worst of the emergency had been averted and, as far as Frank knew from his military training, nothing would stop the blistering, the Dans wanted to go back to the camp to retrieve their packs. Frank accommodated them and, though they were apprehensive about the cost, he agreed to transport them to the hospital for an evaluation. After they had packed their belongings, they loaded into the van again and left for the hospital.

Arriving there, they entered the emergency room. Now familiar with the process, Frank haltingly communicated with the reception clerk. She noted the odd appearance of Dan2, but saw nothing immediately life threatening. Consigning them to a waiting room with the customary stack of paperwork, Frank, grateful that it wasn't his paperwork, handed it to Dan2. He began to wonder if he should even wait when Dr. Albrech happened through and, recognizing Frank and his attendant troupe, stopped to ask Frank if everything was OK with Lacy. Frank replied that she had rested well and thanked him for his concern. He introduced Dan2 and described the encounter with the mustard liquid and described what they had done to minimize the extent of the problem. Dr. Albrech looked briefly at the reddened skin and told Dan2 that he would have some ugly blisters that would appear in the next couple of days. He recommended not popping them and using anti-bacterial ointment and loose bandages when the blisters did pop to prevent an infection.

He said, "Other than what you already have done, unless you have further problems you should be able to care of the injury yourself."

Smiling gratefully, Dan2 stood, thanked the doctor, and walked to the exit followed by the rest of the party. They returned to the van and Frank asked, "Can I drop you guys somewhere?"

The Dans looked at each other and then Dan1 said, "I guess we've had enough of Verdun. How about just dropping us at the highway north. We've talked about touring up into Germany."

Frank headed the van to the north interchange and let the Dans out at the onramp. With a farewell from all and best wishes for a safe trip, they drove away. A last look in the mirror found the Dans walking up the ramp with their thumbs extended and with Dan2 missing one shirt sleeve and pant leg.

John asked his father, "So where should we go to report the bones and the ammunition, Dad?"

Frank replied, "I've been thinking about that, and the only thing that makes sense is to tell the police and let them make the appropriate calls. I doubt that the police investigate old artillery shells, but someone does and they'll know who it is." With that, they headed back toward the police station they had passed near the hospital.

Arriving, they once again unloaded from the van and made their way into the station. A policeman sitting at the desk said, "Bonjour." He had a name badge on his uniform that read, "Sgt. Fourier."

Frank automatically replied, "Bonjour," and feeling slightly ridiculous because he didn't know what came next, said in English, "Do you speak English?"

"Oui," said the officer. "I speak English. How can I help you?"

"We were exploring at Ft. Souville this morning, and within the fort, there was a deep shaft. The boys climbed into the shaft and, at the bottom, they found an old human skeleton."

The officer's eyebrows raised, and he said, "It is prohibited to enter the old fort. Did you not see the sign?"

Frank admitted that they had not, leaving unsaid the fact that they would not have understood the sign had they seen it.

"It happens too frequently that tourists get lost or injured inside of the fort. It is often difficult to find them and get them out. We realize that it is common to go inside, but....." he stopped, perhaps realizing the greater issue and said, "And why do you believe the skeleton was from a human?"

Unable to be restrained, Jarom broke in, "Because it was wearing an ID bracelet and with a tag on its wrist!"

The Sergeant sat up straighter in his chair and looked at the boy. "And you found this skeleton at the bottom of a shaft?"

"Yes," said Jarom, on a roll now. "There were boards and trash at the bottom of the shaft. We were moving them to see what was beneath when we found him."

"And did you read the name on the tag?" questioned the policeman.

"Yes, we did," answered Jarom. "It said, '317 AUXERRE' and then the same thing again only reversed, 'AUXERRE 317'."

"The officer said, "Well it is too bad it has been so long since the Great War. I'm sure that there were loved ones that were waiting for news of this soldier. Now, there will be relatives, perhaps, but after so long they would not have known him. I have access to a database. We shall see if he is present."

He turned the computer monitor on his desk towards him and began typing, and in a few minutes he said, "There were 6 soldiers who died in France between 1914 and 1916 with that last name. We will have to leave it to Le Ministère des Pensions to tell us what the 317 means. This is very valuable information. Thank you for bringing it to us."

"Now where exactly are the remains?" he asked.

Frank first directed him to the Abri Caverne entrance. Then John, who had been chalking the walls on their way in to the fort and was most aware of the turns they had made, described in detail where the shaft was located off the kitchen. The police officer produced a floor plan of the fort. He pointed to the Abri Caverne entrance, and John was able to easily show him where the shaft was.

Frank then began speaking again, more hesitantly this time, saying, "There is one other thing we need to tell you about."

Sergeant Fourier raised his eyebrow and touched his moustache expectantly.

Frank said, "We met two men who were camping outside the fort when we arrived this morning. When we came out of the fort, they had been digging in the remains of a trench and had uncovered many items. They had made a large pile of what appeared to be human bones, mostly arms and legs..."

The policeman interrupted him exasperatedly with, *"Two men,"* he said with disbelief, clearly suspecting that they were making up the Dans.

"Yes, two men...Americans, I think," he said, and then wished that he hadn't. Americans already had a poor enough reputation, but he continued, "They dug up the bones and also several items of unexploded ordinance from the trench. One of them found a German Mustard Gas shell which leaked on him."

The Sergeant stared in disbelief. "So this dangerous chemical was spilled on the man? And what happened to him?"

Frank continued his narrative, "The liquid was spilled on his shirt sleeve and pant leg. I was able to cut them off and wash the contamination, and then we took him to the hospital. The doctor said that we had washed it off in time to prevent serious damage, and the men left hitchhiking along the road to Germany."

"You should know that it is strictly against the law to dig for souvenirs on the battlefields. They are the property of the state. These men have completely disappeared and you are reporting their souvenirs?"

"No," said Frank. "I don't believe that they were taking any souvenirs. All of the items are still there. We felt it was our duty to report the human remains and the ordinance to you...the authorities. The shirt sleeve and the pant leg with the chemical on them are also laying there."

The officer said, "You seem to know much about the chemical mustard gas."

Frank replied, "I am an American Army officer stationed in Mannheim and I am well trained by the Army with regards to chemical weapons. My family and I are on vacation here learning about the great battle."

The policeman stood and said, "Ahhh. Thank you for reporting these things. I will see to it that they are taken care of. Have a pleasant and less eventful vacation. And you are staying where?"

Frank said, "We are at Camping Mairie." He thanked the officer and they turned as a group and walked out the door to the van.

"Dad," Jason said, "I don't think he liked us very much, even though we were trying to do the right thing."

"No, Jason. Probably not. He probably doesn't appreciate our making his life more difficult, even if it *IS* his job and *IS* the right thing.

Chapter 12

Climbing back into the van, Allie asked, "What are we going to do tomorrow?"

The men looked at each other and shrugged. Jarom said, "There are lots more forts we could see, but they are beginning to look the same."

John put in," I guess it will depend on how Mom is feeling. I hope she had a restful day."

Arriving back at the campsite, they were glad to not only observe that the camp had not been trashed, but that Lacy was sitting in a lawn chair in the sun with two of their neighbors. One was the grouchy Frenchman, and the other was a stranger whose campsite was on the other side of theirs. As they got out of the van and somewhat hesitantly walked to the sunny spot their mother had chosen, the neighbors rose and Lacy introduced them.

"Frank, this is our neighbor, Herman," she said indicating the newcomer. "And this is Henri, whom you met the other night. Herman and Henri, this is my husband, Frank, and our children John, Jarom, Jason and Allie." They each formally shook hands in turn as their names were said. "Herman is from Heidelberg, just a few miles from us! What a coincidence! And Henri is from Rouen."

Herman and Henri smiled and sat as Frank retrieved another chair, and the children excused themselves to go to their tents.

To Henri, Frank asked pleasantly "We didn't really speak the other day. Are you just here on holiday?"

"Yes," answered Henri. "I had some business to attend to nearby and decided to stay in the area a few days. My grandfather was in the war not far from here, and my great-grandfather was also in the war here. He is buried in the cemetery of Douaumont. Lacy says you visited it?"

"We did. As I'm sure she told you, we have been visiting the forts and monuments around Verdun. The effort of building them so long ago and manning them, and then fighting the war......is staggering in its magnitude."

"And so sad to have been so wasteful of human life," replied Herman. "After two wars in the last 100 years fought here by our grandfathers and our great-grandfathers, our mothers have raised a generation of pacifists."

Frank smiled. His contact with Germans had shown no lack of national pride, but they no longer had any military aspirations. Their conquest had become an economic one. He said, "The rest of the world has not yet figured that out, I'm afraid. My country continues to fight wars in lands other than our own and with little gain for us. We hope that freedom will be the result for oppressed people, but the results of the wars have been disappointing, I'm afraid. And now that the Cold War is over, we are leaving Germany, and an era is ending."

"An era we are pleased to have end," said Herman. "The Americans have been nothing but generous, but you are right. It is time for your military to go home." Then realizing this may have sounded rude, he added, "But we would love to have you visit anytime."

"I have to say," said Frank, "You both speak excellent English!"

The men smiled and Henri said, "Although they will not always say they speak English, many Europeans do. They all have it in school. I was an exchange student in an American high school."

Herman continued the thought, "And in business I have been required to speak English. My company sent me to our American office for a year, and I have also worked in Australia. I think it is you Americans that do not learn other languages."

Frank replied, "We are often criticized for that. I speak a little German, but poorly. Embarrassed that he might be forced into a demonstration, he turned the conversation to the Henri and said, "Have you seen any of the forts or monuments around Verdun since you have been here?"

"I have been working very hard for the last year and all I have wanted to do for a few days was rest. Tomorrow, I will be a tourist. Your son asked me last night if I had observed anyone in your camp. Has something been damaged?"

Frank answered, "Not really. As far as we could tell, they just knocked over the tents and let the air out of our mattresses as if they were trying to get us to leave. With Lacy here all day today, they have apparently not made another appearance." The thought occurred to him that Herman may have also witnessed the troublemakers, and he asked, "Herman, did you happen to notice anyone in our camp in the last few days?"

Herman frowned and shrugged and finally said, "Perhaps I did yesterday in the morning. I saw a young man approach from across the street there," he said, indicating the direction of Francois' trailer. "I do not know what he was doing and I did not see him damage your camp, but it was peculiar that he was there."

Frank didn't know what to make of that, but it gave them someone to look out for.

"Herman, how did you happen to come to Verdun? Do you also have relatives that were in the war here?"

Answering, Herman said, "As a matter of fact, my great-grandfather was also in Verdun in 1916. He, too, is buried in the cemetery at Douaumont. He, of course, was on the German side. But, when you leave politics behind and are just a soldier in the trenches, you are fighting for your country. I came to honor him for doing that."

"The Ossuary and the cemetery are awe-inspiring and I hope you both will be successful at finding the graves of your great-grandfathers. I expect the 100 year anniversary of 'The Great War' will bring many more descendants like you to the battlefields to remember their forefathers," Frank said thoughtfully. "Will you both go there tomorrow?" he asked.

"I planned to," said Henri. "And you, Herman?"

He answered, "I believe so. Perhaps we can go together?"

"Thank you," said Henri sincerely. "I would enjoy that. And you, Frank and Lacy?"

"No," said Frank. "We have visited there already, and if Lacy is feeling well enough, we were considering packing up and going on toward Paris."

The door on Francois' trailer opened and he stepped out. Seeing the gathering on the other side of the street, he began to walk across, but when he saw the visitors he paused as if to think about joining the party.

Frank called to him, "Francois, please come and join us. We are having a convention of English speakers. Come and meet your neighbors!"

Francois grinned and joined the group. Frank made introductions and found a chair for François. He soon felt at home in the discussion of the histories of their progenitors. Frank and Lacy sat back and enjoyed the discussion which remained in English for their benefit.

The children had not wanted to interrupt the adults and so had begun fixing dinner for themselves and saving leftovers for their parents. As they talked between themselves, they remarked how interesting it was that a group of old people from different countries could quickly find enough in common to be friends in just a few minutes. They watched the faces, smiling, then serious, and then laughing as the group discussion continued, out of their earshot.

When Allie had done the shopping with Lacy, she had convinced her mother of the wisdom of easy-to-fix foods. They had purchased burritos and ramen noodles that the children had prepared for dinner. Allie had chosen a burrito and had warmed it over the stove before eating it. She sat down at the picnic table and took a big bite, but the red meat sauce and beans squirted out of the burrito from the side, completely missing her mouth, but unfortunately not her pants. The red sauce made a huge, oily stain on the front of the pants and, even though she wiped them off as best she could, the greasy spot and the smell of the meat sauce were more than she could tolerate. She excused herself and went to the tent to change.

In the tent, she opened her bag and discovered that there were no more pants. When she was packing, she expected to get two days out of each pair. With the climbing in and out of tunnels, she had soiled them more quickly than she had anticipated, and it was time to do laundry. Looking for the cleanest of the "dirty "pants, she found a pair with only minor smudges. She slipped the grease-stained pair off and the previously worn pair on. She fastened the button on the waistband and zipped the zipper, but something still wasn't right. Her left pocket was lumpy. She stuck her hand into the pocket and her fingers curled around the smooth, flat coins she suddenly remembered putting there. Getting lost and being frightened for her life had completely wiped the memory from her mind, but it all came flooding back to her.

The question was what to do about it. She pulled her hand from her pocket, her fingers clenched around the coins that she still had never laid eyes on. When she opened her hand, she gasped. The coins were perfect. They looked new; and they looked golden! In the lantern light of the tent, the yellow glow of the golden coins took her breath away. Her immediate quandary was if she should tell anyone. She would love to keep them, but she did not know if her parents would allow that. Telling them would surely result in a lecture on honesty and in having them taken away, only to wind up with some French agency or another. Yet, not telling them, was decidedly dishonest.

She closed her fingers around them again and put her hand back in her pocket. She thought, "The coins have been resting there for days; they can just rest there a little longer."

When she got back to her dinner, her appetite was gone. Jarom said, "What kept you? I can't believe a little bit of burrito juice upset you so much. Looking at his shirt, it was obvious that it hadn't upset *him* a bit.

She guiltily picked up her burrito, but her preoccupation was obvious, and Jason asked, "What is the matter?"

That was more than she could handle, and she broke down crying, her head down on her folded arms on the table. The boys looked at each other, not knowing who had cause the flood and not knowing how to stop it.

Jason finally said, "Come on, Allie. Jarom was only kidding!"

Allie lifted her head and said, "Remember when I was lost in the tunnel before you guys came and rescued me?" That obviously didn't require a reply and she went on. "I got lost past the turn to the tunnel with the cave-in. My headlamp was broken and it was completely black dark. I came to what felt like the end of the tunnel and I sat down and my hand fell on a metal box. The box came open and….."

Jarom was interested now, and he hurried her along. "And….what was in the box?"

Instead of answering verbally, she put her left hand into her pocket and then brought it out again. She lay her hand on the table and then, like the petals on a flower opening to the sun, uncurled her fingers to reveal the coins.

The boys were stricken. They could tell immediately that the coins were gold and, though they weren't watchers of the markets, they knew that gold was around $1500 per ounce. That made the coins not only a rarity, but a valuable rarity.

And then, the tears welled up in her eyes again. She said, "So what do I do with them?"

With no hesitation at all, Jason said, "We go back and get the rest of them!"

Allie hadn't even thought that far ahead. She had only been concerned with *these* coins. She hadn't considered all the coins. "No! I mean if I tell Mom and Dad, they will make me give them back, and I like them. I want to keep them. What should I do?"

They knew, of course, as did she what the right thing to do was. And they knew that she would choose the right thing, but that didn't solve the moral dilemma she had at the moment.

John, the voice of maturity and wisdom among her brothers, finally spoke; "Allie, you know you have to tell them and you know that they will do whatever is right. You may not get to keep them, but that doesn't stop us from going to get the rest of them. We don't know who they belonged to, but we have to assume that they were left in that tunnel a long time ago and that nobody else knows about them. I think you should go tell Mom and Dad. Then tomorrow, we should go and get the rest of them so we can turn them in all at once."

The tears left her eyes as she realized that he was right. She had known it all along, of course. The emotional turmoil that she had been going through was just, what she thought of as, her "evil twin" tempting her. Now that her course of action had been resolved, the rest was much easier.

Frank and Lacy were still chatting with the neighbors, but she didn't feel like she could wait. She picked up the coins and put them back into her pocket. Then, she walked over to stand between her mother and father.

She raised her lips to her father's ear and said, 'Daddy, I need to talk with you."

Frank looked at her and was about to tell her that they could talk in a few minutes, after the guests had gone, when he saw the seriousness in her face. He looked over at his wife, and she felt his telepathic signals and turned her head. She saw her daughter and the concerned look on Allie's face and then turned to her and said, "What's the matter, Sweetheart?"

Allie quietly began to retell the tale of being lost in the dark and finding the box that she opened. She pulled her hand from her pocket and as she did so, the conversation in the group stopped and all eyes fell on Allie's hand. She opened her hand to reveal the small, sweaty pile of gold coins.

Frank and Lacy both looked down into the palm of Allie's hand and then, in surprise, Frank picked up one of the coins and read the value and the date. The coin, a 20 Franc piece, was minted in 1912 and had the engraving of a rooster on one side and a man in a hat on the other.

The neighbors were all looking on interestedly, and Frank extended the coin to Francois and asked, "What do you suppose this is worth today?"

Francois said, "I am not a coin collector, but it seems to be gold so it should be worth at least value of the gold, and perhaps much more to a collector." He handed the coin to Henri who studied it for a moment and then nodded his agreement.

Herman did likewise, and then asked, "And where did you find the coins, Allie?"

Embarrassed, and slow in giving an answer, her father said for her, "Allie was in a tunnel beneath one of the forts we visited the other day. She found a box with these in it, but was so frightened at being lost, at the time, that she forgot about it until now."

The obvious question, other than what of the value of the coins were, was if there were more, and Francois asked it. "Allie, were there more coins or just the ones you have here?"

Allie replied, "There was a metal box that had lots of them, but I only brought out a few. It was dark, and I couldn't see them. I could only feel them with my hands."

She looked up into her father's eyes and pleadingly said, "Daddy, can I keep them?"

Frank looked at Lacy, and then said, "I don't know what the laws are, Allie, but we will find out. I suspect that the authorities will say that they are the property of the government."

Francois spoke up, saying, "You are probably correct, but the chance of them actually getting to a museum or the correct agency and not into the pocket of some bureaucrat is small. Perhaps you should consider keeping them."

Henri and Herman kept their opinions to themselves. Henri asked, "Will you go back and get the others?"

The newcomers didn't realize the risks that had been taken to get Allie safely out of the tunnel, and Frank looked at his wife in whose eyes he could once again read disapproval. He said, "If we had the right equipment, I think we could go back safely. We would need a ladder, for sure."

Francois was not pleased that these newcomers were about to invite themselves along on a treasure hunt that he was sure he would be included in.

"I'm sure I could find a ladder at one of the shops in town tomorrow morning, and we could visit the fort again more safely than we were able to the other day," he said to Frank, subtly letting the intruders know that he had been part of the original expedition.

Henri said, "This is all quite exciting, Frank. Would you mind if we came along?"

Frank wasn't sure how this had all gotten out of hand so quickly, but realizing that he had no authority over anyone other than his own family, he said, "I suppose not." And to Francois he said, "What time do you think we might be able to go, Francois?"

Francois grumbled to himself for a moment, and then said, "Perhaps 10 AM"

Frank stood and said, "Well then, I guess we will see you all in the morning. He reached down and closed Allie's fingers over the coins on her palm, helped his wife to her feet, put one arm around her and the other around Allie, and walked back to join the boys at the table.

As they approached the table, conversation stopped and the boys looked up. Jarom asked, "So what do you think, Dad?"

Frank answered, "I think tomorrow will be an interesting day. It seems that Allie is determined to make another visit to her special tunnel."

Lacy was conspicuously silent.

Jarom prodded again, "So can we keep the coins?"

His father replied, "Probably not. Even though it was not exactly digging for souvenirs, I'm pretty sure that the French government will want them back."

"So we're going to go back to the fort tomorrow?" asked Jason.

"Francois says he will get a ladder in the morning so we can get into the tower safely. It should just be a walk in the tunnel to where Allie found the box, and back out again. It seems that even the neighbors want to come along. I guess the attraction of seeing things that have been undisturbed for a century has universal appeal."

"Well, if we have to return the coins, I'll just keep them until tomorrow," she said sadly, patting her pocket.

"Did you guys fix us some dinner too?" asked Frank.

The kids looked up guiltily. Warmed-up burritos were not exactly a prepared meal, but John finally said, "We had burritos....I'll warm some up for you."

Lacy had not had much to eat, but she didn't feel like she was ready for a burrito. She said, "I think I'll have a cup of soup, if it's all the same to you," and she picked up a pan to boil some water.

John took the pan away and said, "Relax, Mom. I'll be glad to get it for you," and Lacy gratefully sat back down.

While they were eating, they discussed their plans for the rest of the week. It was resolved that the next morning Lacy would stay behind and continue her recovery while the rest of the family revisited Fort de Choisel. After everyone was done eating, they put away the food and retired to their tents.

Crawling into her sleeping bag, Lacy was still not happy. The fort that had almost taken her daughter's life was calling them back again. Frank slid into his own bag and reached over to cuddle his wife. Between her cuts and bruises and her mood, she was not very huggable. If for no other reason than he wanted his loving wife back, he was ready to leave Verdun.

The kids crawled into their bags and everyone except John was trying to go to sleep. John's light was still on and he was reading, even though his eyelids were getting heavy. He had noticed earlier that the moon was bright that evening, and he looked at the flap on the front of the tent where he could see the moonlight streaming in. And then something moved in the moonlight, right against the tent. He was sure that someone was there peeking in through the crack. Having no weapon, he reached down to the floor where the football was laying. He nonchalantly tossed it in the air and caught it as he began to sit down on his bed. He snuck one more peek at the door and was sure that he could still make out a dark shape through the crack, silhouetted against the moon. Suddenly, he drew back his arm and threw the ball with all his might at the crack in the tent door and heard a satisfying thud as the ball stuck something solid. He rushed to the door to untie the fastener and stepped out in time to see a dark figure racing away across the street. All that was left was a splash of blood on the tent flap. He wasn't sure why anyone would be spying on them, but he could only imagine that the gold coins might have drawn a thief to their door. Nothing else had changed since the tent had been ransacked in their absence except the gold. *But who*, he thought, *could know about the gold?*

Just to be safe, he stepped over to Allie's bed and found her pants where she had dropped them. He picked them up and stuffed them between his sleeping bag and mattress. *The only way anyone will get those coins tonight is if they take me too*, he thought. He crawled into his bed, turned out the light, and slept uneasily.

Chapter 13

The days had been long and boring. His job was to be the 'undercover' man, and he was 'undercover.' His compatriot was more visible; scouting out targets and setting them up. Penetration and exploitation; that was his job. The two of them had been working together for years now, off and on, and they both made good use of the skills they had developed. Still, it wasn't much fun sitting invisibly behind the scenes, and he was becoming, not only bored, but grouchy. He knew that it was a dangerous state to be in because it made him take careless risks.

When his partner was gone on a scouting trip, he sometimes free-lanced. He worked on technique and sometimes got a bonus that he hadn't counted on. While his partner had been out in the past several days, he had practiced emerging unnoticed and searching target facilities for hidden valuables; exploiting their weaknesses. An unlocked door was an invitation to enter and a careless mistake on the part of the target.

To ease his boredom and sharpen his edge, he peered out through the shaded windows looking for opportunities to strike. He would materialize like a ghost, invisible in manner and action. Even those who were in a position to be watching would not see him. He had practiced his craft on the unsuspecting in the past few days. While targets were absent, he sallied forth to search their dwellings. His incursions created a state of turmoil in their camp. The havoc and fear he caused were his goal. Though he found nothing worthwhile to steal, he felt sure that something would present itself.

His scout had brought him information the evening before. The target had arrived with something of value and had hidden it away. This would be the ultimate test of his skill; to observe while unseen; to infiltrate undetected; and to spirit away a prize. While his compatriot was occupied with trivialities, he slipped away into the darkness. Cloaked within it, he assumed a hidden position outside the target's location to observe; to perceive the location of the valued object.

He assumed the position that he had planned, but something had gone awry. His observation was underway when, without warning, a missile was hurled at his head. It had broken his nose, causing him to bleed and forcing him to retreat in haste lest he be discovered. Yet, versatility in the field was a trait that he aspired to. Though his retreat was hurried, there was no panic; only a carefully measured and smoothly executed response to an unfavorable occurrence. The unexpected can arise in even the most well-planned maneuver.

Chapter 14

When morning came, John was not awakened by the sun; neither by breakfast cooking, or by his brothers jumping on his bed. All those things had happened in the recent past, but that morning he was awakened by his sister whimpering about her missing pants.

"John, Jarom, Jason.....Wake up!" she said. "Someone took my pants!"

Finally coming awake, John realized that he was the guilty party. "Allie," he called softly. "Come here...I have them over here."

"Why did you take my pants, John?" she asked.

He told her about the Peeping Tom that he had caught the night before. He explained that he couldn't see how anyone else could have known about the gold coins, but that he wasn't taking any chances. He rolled over and pulled her well-pressed pants out from beneath his sleeping bag. She slipped them on and then put her hand in the pocket and pulled it inside out. The pocket was empty!

John said, "I don't see how...."

Smiling smugly, Allie said, "I put them in the bottom of my sleeping bag because I didn't want anyone to steal them either!"

He said, "I guess great minds think alike."

It was only 7:30 and the rest of the camp was still quiet. With the sun lighting the day, John looked in the direction he had seen the Peeper run. It seemed that the Peeper had run across the street.

John knew that they were probably leaving that day, but he was still angry that someone had trashed their camp three times. And then he had seen a Peeping Tom! He had drawn blood!

He put his musings on hold when he saw the camp kitchen laid out on the picnic table. He guessed that it must be his turn to fix breakfast, especially if he was going to eat any time soon. He opened up the ice chest and got out the eggs and milk and bread. He lit the fire on the stove and was soon cooking French toast, thinking it was only appropriate given their location. Allie got out the paper plates and cups, milk, orange juice and yoghurt. When everything was ready, including the syrup, Allie was dispatched to bring her parents to the table while John went to get Jarom and Jason.

A few minutes later, with only low-level grumbles being heard, the family sat down to breakfast. They had their morning devotional together and began to plan the day.

Just as breakfast was ending, Francois came out of his trailer and Frank waved to him. Walking to the middle of the street, Frank asked Francois if he would like company in going to get the ladder. Francois said he would and he and Frank climbed into the van and headed off to town. They arrived at a hardware store that had just opened and Francois told the proprietor that they were looking for an extendable ladder. He showed them long extension ladders, foldable ladders, step ladders, and finally a collapsible ladder that was just what they needed. The legs of the ladder were aluminum tubing, and each length slid down inside the one below it. Fully extended, the ladder was nearly 15 feet long; long enough to reach most of the way up the side of the observation tower.

They bought the ladder and drove back to the campground. The children were ready to go, headlamps and water bottles in their backpacks. It was 10:00 AM as they were loading into the van when both Henri and Herman walked up from their respective trailers.

"Bon Jour," greeted Henri.

Not to be outdone, Herman greeted them with, "Guten Morgen!"

Now that their national pride had been satisfied, they continued on in English. "Do we need to take another vehicle?" asked Herman. "I could drive if necessary."

Frank began to count noses. The Transit held 9, including the driver, and they numbered eight. "It might be a little tight in the back," he said, "but we should all fit. Do you have flashlights or headlamps?" he asked. Herman had a flashlight, but Henri admitted that he did not. Since Lacy wasn't coming, her headlamp was available, and Frank went to retrieve it. By the time he returned, everyone was in the van with Francois riding "shotgun". Frank got in and started the engine, and they were once again covering the now-familiar roads on their way to Fort de Choisel.

After parking outside the fence, they quickly exited the van. Packing their gear and the ladder, they hiked down through woods to where they could crawl under the fence. While the ladder was quite back-packable with a rope sling on each side, it was bulky enough that it required the coordinated action of lifting the fencing and enlarging the width of the hole to maneuver it under. After the ladder was finally past the obstacle, they donned their packs for the hike up to the fort.

After several minutes of walking through the woods, they came to the moat. Henri and Herman had not seen one of the old forts that had not been sanitized for tourists, and they were first impressed by the overgrowth of vegetation that was that was gradually burying the fort like a Mayan pyramid in the jungle.

To most easily find the tower in the dense woods, they decided it would be simpler to drop into the moat and locate the landmarks from their previous visit and then climb back out and cross directly to it. They made their way down the side of the moat with Jason giving a running commentary to Henri and Herman about the moat and the fort and its defenses. They came to where they had climbed back out of the moat before and repeated their ascent with the two additions as well as the ladder. John, who was carrying the ladder, was starting to drag a bit, but as he came out of the ditch and started off through the trees, he picked up the pace, eager to climb into the tower again.

Arriving at the observation post, John and Jarom set about extending the ladder and then leaned it up against the side of the tower. Jarom was first up the ladder. From the top rung, his head and shoulders were above the platform and, with a little acrobatics, he was able to climb onto it. John followed him up and also demonstrated his gymnastic talent. Allie followed and, with her brothers each giving her a hand, leapt up on to the platform. A little shorter than his brothers, Jason also needed two hands up.

Francois climbed up and was grateful for the help of the boys, and the other men followed in turn. Jarom directed them onto the stairway as the platform wouldn't hold everyone. Lamps at the ready and Allie leading, they started down the stairs.

The rusty spiral staircase creaked a bit but held together as the men descended around it. They came to the flights of concrete steps and all were soon at the bottom. The light noticeably dimmer, they became more dependent upon their lamps. As they made their way down the tunnel, the lamps became the only source of light.

Allie leading and Frank behind her, they continued single-file along the passage. On the right they passed the opening of the Travaux 17 tunnel that had collapsed on them only a few days before. Examining the condition of the tunnel they were in from an engineering perspective, Frank noticed that the walls and roof were poured concrete, and he pronounced it safe for their travel.

Allie continued to walk, nervous that there did not seem to be an end to the tunnel. She distinctly remembered coming to a solid wall that she sat down in front of when she found the box, but there was no wall before her. She could not exactly remember how far she had walked in the dark a few days before, but she thought that she had surely had come far enough. Without the landmark she was looking for however, she kept walking. The others were trailing her but, like a team of Alaskan sled-dogs, when you're not the leader the scenery never changes, and they could do little else *but* follow.

10 minutes of walking, and then 20 and then 25 minutes and the tunnel opened up to another staircase. Francois, Henri and Herman could tell that there was a problem, but they did not know what it was. Never having seen the inside of a fort, Henri and Herman were in a wonderland. Francois and the boys escorted the new explorers up the stairs they had come to so they could have a look.

Francois said, "This is not Fort de Choisel. We have walked too far and I believe that through the Travaux 17 tunnel, we have come to Fort du Chana which is located about 300 meters south of

Choisel." He continued his monologue as they ascended the steps, leaving Frank and Allie to talk for a few minutes.

Tearfully, Allie said to her dad, "I don't know where it went! We had to have walked right past the box because the tunnel doesn't go anywhere else. I couldn't have come this far!"

Frank tried to calm his daughter, saying, "Honey, you obviously found the coins before. Today, something is different. All these people make you nervous, of course, but let's think this through. What was different before?"

"Well, I didn't have a light and I couldn't see anything."

"How did you find your way in the tunnel without a light?" he asked.

She closed her eyes to imagine what she had done. She held her left hand to the side and her right in front of her and said, "I dragged my left hand along the tunnel wall and kept my right hand in front of me so I wouldn't walk into anything."

"And then what happened," he prompted?

"Pretty soon my right hand ran into a wall and I sat down and there was the box."

Frank said, "I'm going to tell them to explore this fort for a little while and you and I will go back and try it again without the lights." He ran up the stairs and told the others that they should come back along the tunnel in about 30 minutes, and then he returned. He and Allie started walking back along the tunnel.

Knowing where they were going, they walked more quickly than they had before and soon were back at the opening to the collapsed tunnel that led to Fort de Choisel. Frank turned them around and turned off the lights. With Allie in the lead, they began walking through the coal-black darkness.

With her right hand in front, Allie dragged her left hand along the wall and, in only a few minutes, her right hand found the end of the tunnel. Mystified, she snapped on the headlamp and, after few seconds for her eyes to adjust, she saw that she had missed a small and almost camouflaged opening to her left. Her left hand dragging on the wall had led her into the opening and turned her body enough that her right hand found the other side of the opening. It had seemed to be the end of the tunnel, even though the tunnel went on. She looked down where she'd sat a few days before, and there, inside the small opening, sat the box. Frank watched her lift the lid, move it away, and gasped involuntarily as the light glinted off the faces of the coins in the box. There were coins in several denominations, each in their own compartments, but the coins that caught Frank's attention were made of gold. The box had a deep tray that held loose coinage and beneath were the coins stored in rolls. The coins on the deeper level mirrored those in the tray above, and Frank's quick calculation left him believing that there were well over one thousand gold coins contained in the box, not to mention those of less noble origin. The collector's value notwithstanding, the price of gold bullion in the $1500 an ounce range made the box and its contents valuable.

Allie tried to explain what had happened, but Frank understood without the telling. "This was," he thought, "kind of a special daddy/daughter moment," and he reached out and curled his arm around her and kissed her on the top of the head.

Allie tried to count the coins but they weren't evenly stacked and the rows were uneven. Together they decided that it didn't really matter and was, maybe, better that they didn't know. They were committed to turning them in to the police station in Verdun and, with that complete, they would finally be off to EuroDisney.

They could hear the echoes in the tunnel as the rest of the company approached from Fort du Chana. The voices and footsteps grew louder and, in a few minutes and with Jarom at the front of the line, they appeared. He saw their headlamps and the cul-de-sac in the wall and he, too, understood that they had all walked right past the cache. With some effort Allie lifted the box into her lap and slid the lid off, and Jarom and Jason and all that could crowd around her in that small space eagerly looked at the lost treasure of the fort.

Because the space was so tight, Frank said, "Let's walk back up the tunnel to the tower and we can all have a closer look," and without argument the troop fell back into line and filed up the tunnel. When they had all gone past, Frank helped Allie up and then, because it was a bit heavy, took the box from her with the lid in place and retraced their steps again to the tower.

When they had climbed the staircase to the tower platform, they found that Francois, Henri, and Herman had already climbed down the ladder and were steadying it on the ground for Jason who was being lowered to the top rung of the ladder by his brothers. Allie was next, getting her footing on the top rung and then backing a step down the ladder to where she could let go of her brothers' hands and grab on. On his stomach, Frank edged off the platform and found the top of the ladder with his feet. He took two steps down and then received the box from John who handed it to him. Finally, the older brothers made it all look too easy and in a moment they were all on the ground.

There was plenty of room for all to see, so Frank set the box down on the remains of a concrete pad that had once adorned the site and each, in turn, fondled the coins until they were satisfied. Then by common consent, Frank put the lid on the box, picked it up, and they all made their way back to the van.

Frank opened the rear hatch and put the box on the floor along with the ladder, closed the hatch, and everyone piled in for the ride back to Camping Mairie. They bumped across the old road beside the farm field and were soon on the pavement. It took only a few more minutes to arrive at the campsite and, pulling up into his spot, Frank shut off the engine. The explorers disembarked and, as Lacy came over to greet them, he opened up the hatch and waited for Allie to come and lift the lid so her mother could see the treasure. They all took one more look and then Allie replaced the lid. Frank closed the hatch on the van.

"We all discussed last night what should be done with the coins," said Frank to the assembled group. In the abstract, looking at only a few coins, it wasn't hard to imagine keeping them as souvenirs. Now that we've seen the entire collection, it is easier to see that it does belong to the French government. We plan to leave Verdun today, so we will pack up our belongings and then, on our way out of town, we'll stop at the police station and turn them over to the authorities there. We will trust them to do the right thing with the coins."

He didn't see any disbelieving faces, but he could imagine that some of the others might be thinking that he would simply abscond with the treasure. To allay any possible concerns, he added, "If any of you would like to accompany us to the police station, we would be grateful for your added witness there."

Francois, Henri and Herman each nodded their assent, said their farewells and thanks, and walked back to their trailers.

To the children, Frank said, "I hope you're not disappointed about giving the coins up to the French government."

Jarom replied, "No, Dad. After seeing the whole box and how they were apparently left there, I guess it's the right thing to do."

The others agreed and Frank turned to his own tent and the children to theirs. It took some time to flatten the mattresses, roll up the sleeping bags, and pack away the clothes. Before they were done, Lacy noticed that it was past lunch time and, recovering from her injuries, set about fixing lunch for her family. She called her family to eat and they arrived without delay. They made their own sandwiches, each chose a can of soda pop to drink, and they enjoyed their last meal together at Camping Mairie.

Lunch over, they went back to their tents to finish their packing and to strike the tents.

Chapter 15

His partner had finally returned from his scouting trip and reported that the American targets had found a box full of valuable coins. He had been waiting for days for a worthwhile mission and he finally had been given one. The confusion he had created in the past few days would only plant the seed that someone from outside the camping spot might be responsible for once again attacking them. At the time, he had only thought of his excursions as entertainment and training, but his actions had been prescient.

His partner was pessimistic about his chances of bringing back the box undiscovered, but he lived a charmed life. He was a skilled operative! It was really hardly a challenge to operate undetected in this environment among the completely unsuspecting.

He looked out the shaded window of the trailer that served as their headquarters. He watched the American targets talking together and then they all went inside their tents. His companion had complained of a headache and was lying down, so he cracked the door and slipped out. He saw no one on the street so he crossed and, standing behind the American van, was out of the line of sight from either of the tents. He pushed the release button on the rear hatch of the van and, holding it against the gas-jets that would spring it up, eased it open only as far as it took to reach into the opening and extract the metal box. He noiselessly closed the hatch and turned to make his way back across the street. "The Invisible Man," he thought to himself as he nonchalantly walked to the other side carrying the heavy box. Floating up over the curb, "The Invisible Man" caught his toe and tripped. He dropped the box and it crashed noisily to the ground. The lid bounced partially off and a hundred coins rolled out onto the sidewalk. Cursing to himself but remaining the picture of calm, he knelt and began to pick them up. No witnesses were visible on either end of the street, and he began to think of the misfortune as one of the unpredictable occurrences that requires flexibility in planning and execution.

He heard the door on his own trailer open and saw his companion's face turn angry when he saw the spilled coins. "Hurry up!" said his companion, "and don't miss any of them! Get them inside quickly! I thought I told you that this was too risky!"

He stood and took one more casual look around, the picture of innocence. Everything appeared to be in order and there were still no witnesses. He picked up the box and moved carefully into the trailer.

Chapter 16

With the pile of baggage stacked beside the van waiting to be stowed, John climbed on top, opened the clamshell, and his brothers and father began tossing him the tents, stove, sleeping bags, and other gear they would not need on their trip.

Frank figured it was only a 3 hour drive to EuroDisney. That should allow them time to deal with the police in Verdun and still be able to find a camping spot outside the EuroDisney Park. They would spend the night there and then the whole next day in the Park. He hoped that they would be able to go into Paris the following day and see the Eiffel Tower and the Arc De Triomphe and maybe the Notre Dame Cathedral. Then the next day, maybe the Louvre.....He was still lost in thought when he heard noise from the back of the van.

"Dad," yelled John, "What did you do with the box? Didn't you leave it back here?"

Frank walked around to the back of the van and looked into the empty space. He turned to the rest of the family, "Did any of you move the box from the back of the van?"

He was answered with a chorus of NOs, and he began to panic. He was sure that the box had been secure in the van. That was why he had left it there. Not only would it be terrible to have it go missing, but he would never be able to convince his neighbors that he had not hidden it away to avoid turning it over to the police.

"John," he said sharply. "Go and ask the neighbors to come over. We have got to find that box!"

John did as he was told and, in a few minutes, Henri, Herman and then Francois arrived.

Frank addressed them: "While we were packing our gear, someone apparently got into the back of the van and took the box of coins. No one even knew they were there except us. Did any of you see someone around the van? On the street?" He was met with shaking heads.

"Did you hear a vehicle come down the street?" He was grasping at straws and he said, "Do you have any other ideas about what might have happened?"

Francois' face darkened and he was becoming visibly upset. He said, "Yes, I have an idea. I thought we had become friends and I hate to come to this conclusion, but those coins are very valuable, I imagine. Turning them into the authorities may be the honest thing to do, but if they were 'lost' you would not be able turn them in as you have promised to do. In fact they may remain 'lost' until you happen to 'find' them when you return to Germany!"

Frank said, "That is ridiculous!" dismissing the idea entirely. "That is something we absolutely would *not* do!" he said exasperatedly. Frank was used to being in charge and having the answers, but being accused and having no evidence for his defense made him feel completely impotent.

"I don't know what to do now. I don't know if there would be any value in searching in this area. Would you help us talk to the others that are camping along this street? You would be able to explain that we are looking for thieves in French while I could not. I will go and talk to the manager of the campground and see if he has any seen any strangers or has any other suggestions. If we can't come up with something, I suppose the next thing would be to call the police, though I imagine they will hardly be pleased since we have removed something of value from one of the forts."

Herman said, "I will be happy to help, but it is amazing to me to think that it could have disappeared into thin air with witnesses all around. Still, I don't believe that you would have taken the box."

Henri added, "I am also surprised to find it missing, but it is clear that you did not have to invite us along on your excursion or even share the discovery with us. After all of that, it is difficult to believe you would have arranged the theft. If that was what you had intended to do, you could have done it much more simply by going back to the fort alone. I will do what I can to help. Where should I begin searching?"

They both looked at Francois who shrugged and nodded his willingness to help. Frank, looked back at Francois but said nothing.

Finally Francois spoke, "Perhaps it is impractical to think that you have stolen the box. Let's begin talking to the other neighbors."

Playing quarterback, Frank suggested that Herman begin on the other side of the street past Francois' trailer and then work back toward their camp. He asked Henri to begin at the other end of the street and to work back from that direction, and then asked Francois to accompany him to the office to talk to the manager.

They all began in their assigned spots, talking to the people at each campsite in turn; asking about thefts and strangers. No one reported anything suspicious. Francois and Frank talked to the manager for several minutes, but he had seen nothing out of the ordinary and had no ideas of what they might do. They turned to walk back to the campsite.

Herman, passing in front of Francois' trailer on his return from the end of the street, saw something shiny on the ground. He bent over and picked up a gold coin with a rooster on one side. Surprised, he fell to one knee and was looking through the grass growing there when Henri walked up. He had just finished canvassing his end of the street and noticed Herman looking for something in the grass.

"What did you find, Herman?" asked Henri.

"I believe you call this a clue," he said. "Next to the sidewalk, I saw the sun reflecting off of a shiny object in the grass. I picked it up and discovered it to be a gold coin like we were shown last evening. The only way that I can imagine that it came to be here is if the thief dropped it somehow."

Henri joined Herman on his knees looking through the grass and, in a moment, they had turned up several other coins of different denominations with mint dates in the 1920's and 30's. It could not be a coincidence that such old coins were all found here together. It had to be the work of the thief.

Herman asked, "How do you suppose he might have dropped the coins?"

Henri answered, "It is logical to assume that he didn't drop the coins, but dropped the box and these were not retrieved. Imagine the panic he must have felt at his exposure! With so many potential witnesses here and for him to have escaped so cleanly, his destination must have been very near."

Both men began to look at the area from where they were. The last known place the thief had been was where they were kneeling. They looked down the street in both directions, but their eyes finally came back to the trailer in front of them. Just then, they heard a noise in the trailer as if someone were walking around inside.

"Francois is with Frank. See them coming back from the office," said Henri pointing toward the men at the other end of the street. "The thief may have hidden out of sight and then taken refuge in Francois' trailer while we were all out searching for him!"

"And it sounds as if he might be in this trailer right now!" exclaimed Herman.

They stood and walked to the door of Francois' trailer, Henri reaching out with his fist and pounding on the door. They listened, but there was no sound. They both knew that they had heard movement a few seconds ago, and Henri pounded on the door again. He tried the door as Herman began to walk around to the back of the trailer.

Chapter 17

Maintaining covert surveillance, he continued to watch through the curtained window. He watched the big German coming down the street and stop immediately in front of the trailer. "No need to panic," he told himself. "It is surely a coincidence that he should stop there." The German held up a shining sliver of sunlight and then he was joined by the Frenchman from across the street. They were both searching through the grass and recovered some of his coins! They were examining them closely and then looking up and down the street. Suddenly, he worried that as close as they were he might be visible behind the curtain, so he stepped back a pace and the floor creaked.

His calm began to desert him when he saw both men rise and come to the door. He heard the hammering on the door and froze. The hammering stopped and he stood stalk-still. The pounding began again and he moved back to the other end of the trailer under the cover of the din.

He had been examining the contents of the box when he had noticed the activity in the street and had gone to the window to watch. He began to gather up the coins and replace them in the box when he heard the doorknob being tried. Looking down the hall, he saw the door beginning to open and, putting into action the escape plan he had plotted many times, he pushed open the emergency escape window over the kitchen table and rolled out through it, carrying the box with him and leaving the remaining coins on the counter.

The table was a good 6 feet above the ground outside and, as he rolled through the window, he fell to the ground landing clumsily but still holding the box. He began to run away toward the woods when he saw the German begin running after him. He was fast, but he was still carrying the heavy box. The German was faster, and he sensed that if he didn't abandon the box, he would be apprehended. He dropped the box and it crashed to the ground, coins going in every direction. He expected the German to stop for the box, but he didn't. His felt his forward progress halted when the German's weight drove him to the ground as he was tackled around the waist.

Chapter 18

Looking down the main hall into the kitchen of the trailer, Henri saw a man jump out of a window on the back of the trailer and take off running carrying the missing box! He wasn't sure of the details, but he was sure that the man was escaping, so he ran back to the front door to chase after him.

Meanwhile, Herman had come around the end of the trailer and heard the landing of heavy feet on the ground and the shake of coins in a metal box. He looked up to see a man regain his balance and take off running away from the trailer carrying the missing box! Though he was starting from behind, he took up the pursuit. He could see the box was slowing the runner down, and he increased his speed to catch him. He saw the man glance over his shoulder and then drop the box. The lid came off and he watched the coins scatter on the ground, but the German didn't slacken his pace. He was already close enough to launch a flying tackle which brought the fleeing man to the ground. A moment later, Henri ran up and, surprising both men, pulled handcuffs from his belt beneath his shirt tail and applied them expertly to the wrists of the sacked stranger.

They all sat there a moment catching their breath. Henri asked Herman, "Where did you learn to tackle like that?"

Herman answered, "It has been a while, but I lived in Australia for a time and learned to play rugby." Then with a credible Australian accent, "How'd I do, mate?"

Henri laughed and when Herman began to question him about the handcuffs, he said, "I'll explain all of that in a few minutes, but I think we still have one more thief to take care of."

He stood and pulled the captive to his feet and the three began walking back toward the trailer. As they reached it, Francois and Frank came around the corner and, to their surprise, Henri and Herman were leading a third man along in handcuffs.

"Who's this," sputtered Francois. "And why is he in chains?"

Leaving the thief in Herman's custody for a moment, Henri reached out and grabbed for Francois' wrists. Francois jerked them away and said, "What are you playing at. You've no reason to grab hold of me. What do you think you're doing?"

Watching Francois closely, Henri reached into his coat pocket and brought out a badge case which he opened to reveal a shield that identified him as a member of Sûreté, the French National Police Force. There was general astonishment from the group, and Henri said to Francois, "You are under arrest for attempted theft and other charges which will be forthcoming." He turned to the other man and repeated, you too, are under arrest for attempted theft and other charges that will be forthcoming."

Francois said loudly, "You have no right to do this. I have done nothing wrong and I am being treated as a criminal. I will have charges brought against you! I want to talk to my attorney!"

Henri replied, "If there has been a mistake, I assure you that you will receive a most humble and sincere apology. But I also assure you that there is no mistake."

Henri grabbed Francois' right arm and held it behind his back without tension, but in a threatening position that could easily be made painful. He said, "I regret that I have only one pair of handcuffs with me. Herman, if you would please help me to escort these gentlemen across the street where I can make them more comfortable and secure, we will call the police for reinforcements and I can perhaps explain what is going on."

Herman did as he was asked and, when they arrived, Henri unlocked his car and retrieved another set of handcuffs which he applied to the wrists of Francois, interlocked with those of his companion. He invited them to sit down and, when they obeyed, he took out his cell phone and placed a call to the local police station.

After a hurried conversation in French, he ended the call and then turned to Frank. By this time the rest of the family had arrived and were trying to take in what they saw before them. Seeing their friend, Francois, in handcuffs locked together with a stranger they did not know was difficult for them to process, but they gave Henri and their father the benefit of the doubt and waited for an explanation.

The explanation was not immediately forthcoming, however. Henri said, "I beg of you. There is one more thing of great importance that must be done before the arrival of the police to avoid problems for you. I'm afraid that these men have attempted to steal the cash-box that you recovered from the fort this morning and, in the process, it was spilled over the ground. It is behind Francois' trailer and it would be most unfortunate if it were not intact when the police arrive."

Frank could see that it might indeed be awkward if the cash box they had brought out of the fort under somewhat questionable circumstances had been damaged before they could turn it in to the proper authorities. The authorities might not be amused, so Frank and his four children hurried around to the back of the trailer where they found the cash box open and the tray separated from it and empty. The box itself still held most of the rolls of coins, and they quickly set about retrieving, sorting, and stacking the coins back in the tray. There were 7 different compartments for the different denominations, and the bulk of the coins were back in their usual places within a few minutes. They moved the box aside and then went through the grass on their hands and knees to pick up any coins that they might have missed and, finding only a very few, finally put the tray in the box and closed it.

Frank picked it up and together they walked back around to the street just in time to see a police car pulling up. While the James were still a distance off, Henri showed his police identification to the officers and had a quick discussion with them. They climbed out and opened the back door of their sedan.

Francois began to protest again very loudly, "I am innocent and I want an attorney." To the officers directly, he said, "These men have falsely accused me of a crime and I demand to be released."

The two officers looked at each other and rolled their eyes. Taking a handcuff key from his pocket, one of the policemen helped Francois and his companion stand and, unlocking one of Francois' wrist locks, he separated the men. Then, to Francois' complete indignation, he locked the cuff back around his wrist. He then helped the protesting Francois to sit in the back of the patrol car while his partner seated the other man on the opposite side. After the men were settled, they closed both doors and turned to Henri.

Chapter 19

Together in the back of the police car, Francois turned angrily to his companion. In rapid French, he said "I told you it was too risky! We came here not to work but to take a vacation from work. We have been so successful that we did not need to work here! And now we are ruined. You with your spy game; refusing to come out and see where our relatives lived!"

"Francois, do not lecture me! It is because of my skills that we have been so successful. Do you think you could really survive on your pension? What we have put away....."

"Will be for nothing!" Francois finished for him. "We have been caught. Where do you intend to spend all of the money? In prison?"

"We are not in prison yet. I told you it was a mistake to become so friendly with the Americans. They had nothing to steal. It was only by chance that they found a treasure, and it was too good to pass up."

"If it caused us to be caught, it was NOT too good to pass up. What were you thinking, cousin?" asked Francois incredulously. "

"Just like in every other place that we have worked, I was thinking that our discipline and skill would bring us more riches. It was you who ruined us with your 'friends', the Americans. Why could you not see that getting too close to them would bring us trouble?"

Francois looked at his cousin once again. They had been in business together for a long time, and he knew that he would not win an argument with him. He also knew that they should say nothing now to each other or to the police. He turned away into silence, waiting for the opportunity to talk to their lawyer. He knew they would be back in business soon enough.

Chapter 20

Just then, the James family, including Lacy, walked up. The police officer and Frank recognized each other. They, of course, had met in the station a few days before when Frank had been reporting the bones and armaments that had been uncovered at Ft. Souville. The policeman looked at Frank with some disdain, and Frank did not look forward to the telling of his own tale today. He was sure he would hear about it being forbidden to enter the fort and illegal to take souvenirs but, before they could begin a discussion, Henri began to talk.

"Three years ago, many local police departments in different areas of France received reports from tourists camping in campgrounds that they had been robbed while they were absent. Because the times of the alleged thefts never overlapped, we suspected that they were being carried out by a single thief. The problem was that he moved around the country and we were always following the thefts, sometimes only by hours. We French regard ourselves as good hosts and the government did not want to have negative publicity that would discourage tourists from visiting. I was assigned to find the thieves and stop the thefts."

"I interviewed the proprietors of camping facilities, the tourists who were robbed, and other people camping close by. I could not find a pattern but eventually discovered a repeated description of a camping trailer that always seemed nearby when a theft occurred. We asked the police in the entire nation to be on the look-out for the trailer, but there were many of the same style. A week ago we got lucky. Someone noticed the license number of a trailer that left a campground just before a theft was reported. When we compared the license and the style of the camper, we had a match. We then had to find the trailer in a campground so we could apprehend the thief."

"An alert patrolman had seen our license request and noticed the trailer on the highway between Paris and Verdun. He tracked the trailer to this campground, and I brought my own trailer and parked it across the street in an undercover operation. I watched the trailer carefully, and then your family arrived," he indicated to Frank. "I am sorry for the rude reception I offered you on your arrival, but I'd hoped you would find another camping space so that my surveillance would be unobstructed. That is why I parked the way I did and spoke to you only in rude French. When Francois intervened on your behalf, there was nothing else to be done, and I moved my trailer."

"Your family seemed to begin a friendship with 'Francois', and I continued to watch you come and go but nothing appeared suspicious. I began to think that I might have been wrong. Then, while you and Francois were gone, I noticed from behind my curtains that the door opened on his trailer and a man I did not recognize stepped out. I observed while he surreptitiously went to your campsite. He went through each tent and, apparently finding nothing, knocked them both down. I suspected that he had found nothing of value and was expressing his discouragement. Because I felt that Francois was the bigger thief, however, I waited for evidence of his wrongdoing."

"Francois continued to come and go with your family and it was clear that you had begun to trust him. It was also becoming clear to me how the two actually worked as a team: Francois would create trust with a family and then his companion would be able to go through their belongings at his leisure with no risk. He was actually very good; almost invisible in his ordinariness."

"The next day when your family left with Francois, I was surprised to see his partner go through your camp again. I concluded that he wanted you to leave so another person might camp there that would be more profitable for him, so he was making it uncomfortable for you to stay. You, however, didn't leave as he expected. Even after a third time upsetting your tents, you remained."

"Finally, Allie introduced us to the treasure that she had found in the fort." With that, Sergeant Fourier's eyes opened wider and he said, "Treasure you found in the fort?"

Henri said, "We will cover all of that as well," and the sergeant put his suspicions aside for a moment while Henri continued. When Francois saw the coins that Allie showed us a few nights ago, the larceny in his heart became uncontrollable. He went back to his trailer and must have discussed it with his compatriot. He knew that Allie had the coins in the pocket of her pants, and Francois sent out his sneak-thief to steal the coins while she slept. I watched him leave the trailer and skulk across the street. A few minutes he returned but, from his manner, he appeared injured and unsuccessful."

"And if you want evidence that it was the same man," interrupted John, "look at his face." I saw his outline through the crack in the tent door and I threw my football at his face as hard as I could. It must have done some damage!"

Interested now in witnesses and evidence, Henri walked around to the opposite side of the patrol car and opened the door. He looked closely at the man's face as the man curiously looked back at him. Sure enough, his nose was swollen, bruised, and crooked. There were traces of blood and mucous on his lip. Henri smiled and shut the car door and returned to the group to continue the story.

"You're right," he reported. "I will have to make sure that we get a close-up photograph of his face and record your statement. It will be evidence of one more crime. Peepers are not let off lightly here."

"This afternoon when we returned from the fort, the only ones who were aware of where the cash-box was located were your family," he said gesturing to Frank and the children, "Herman, Francois, and myself. When John summoned us and Francois finally came out of his trailer, and you revealed that the box was missing, it seemed that the pool of suspects was very small. I knew I had not taken the box, I did not believe Herman had, and my suspicions of Francois were confirmed completely when he accused you of hiding the coins in order to keep them rather than turn them over to the government."

"You would never have involved any of us if you had intended to keep the coins. Still, it was possible that someone else might have seen you place the box in the back of the van, so I helped with the search. However, when Herman found the little golden rooster coin, all of the pieces of the puzzle fit together and I knew that if we could just find evidence that Francois had the coins in his trailer, he could be convicted."

"I needed a reason to enter his trailer, and his partner gave us one when we heard him moving about. We knocked on the door and he crashed out through the emergency exit window in the back with the coins and we caught him red-handed, as your police shows say. I arrested him and Francois, the police arrived, and now you know the whole story. Francois and his partner are the notorious campground thieves, and with your help, they have been captured."

Sergeant Fourier nodded his understanding, but then turned to Frank and said, "I thought we had discussed the fact that entrance into the forts was prohibited, and that it was illegal to remove souvenirs."

Frank looked at him guiltily, and after Sergeant Fourier had let all of them squirm for a moment, he said, "Well, perhaps we could demonstrate your good faith by the fact that you are returning the state's property." Sergeant Fourier did not mention that entry into the forts was officially prohibited but no one was ever prosecuted. There were just too many of the old structures to patrol. As long as people weren't injured, the exploration was tacitly allowed. He said, "May I see the box?"

Frank picked it up and opened the lid. Sergeant Fourier gasped when he saw all the coins neatly arrayed as they must have been left so long ago. He was, as everyone was, most enamored of the gold pieces. "And how did you come to find this box in a fort that has been explored a thousand times?"

Frank began to tell the tale, and told how Allie had inadvertently come upon it when she had been lost in the dark tunnel. Allie, who had listened intently to the whole exchange, reached into her pocket and withdrew the coins that had led all of them to the discovery and capture of the thieves. She held out her hand and dropped the coins into the Sergeant's palm and said, "Here are the coins that I found in the tunnel. I didn't mean to steal them. I didn't even know what they were until I remembered them in my pocket last night and showed them to everyone."

Sergeant Fourier looked at her trembling lip and then at the six coins he held in his palm, and finally at the box that had been recovered for the French government. And then he said, "Thank you, my dear. You have been most honest and on behalf of France, I thank you." Then he took her hand and opened the fingers and dropped the coins back into her palm and said, "And on behalf of France, I present these remembrances to your family, one for each of you, to thank you for your part in recovering this treasure and in capturing these thieves."

With a huge grin, Allie jumped up and hugged the Sergeant and said, "Oh thank you. I really did want one just to keep for a souvenir."

The policemen got into the car with the cash box and drove off for the station. Henri shook their hands and drove off following in his own car. Herman shook their hands and thanked them for all of the excitement. He said that it wasn't exactly the relaxation he was expecting, but that it was far better.

Everything was packed but had not yet been put away in the van, so John resumed his position on top. He piled a few remaining things into the clamshell and closed and secured it. Jarom finished loading the rest of the luggage into the hatch, and it was time to go. They climbed into their customary seats, Frank started the engine, and said, "EuroDisney, anyone?" and they drove off.

Resources

Photo of a typical French "squatter".
http://www.jarrelook.co.uk/Urbex/Verdun/Ouvrage%20de%20Fr oideterre/May%202011/Barracks/Verdun_Froideterre_May_2011_barrac ks_08.jpg

A Map of the location of the World War I Forts and installations around Verdun
http://www.jarrelook.co.uk/Urbex/Verdun/Fort_locations.jpg

The Battle of Verdun
http://en.wikipedia.org/wiki/Battle_of_Verdun

Good analysis of why the forts at Verdun were constructed, Pictures and write up of several of the Verdun area forts:
http://www.jarrelook.co.uk/Urbex/Verdun/Verdun.htm

A French site of the forts of Verdun, as well as the rest of France (Select English in the drop-down box in the website header)
http://fortiffsere.fr/verdun/
Photo of the markers of the Voie Sacree
https://www.flickr.com/photos/mlautard/14194126334/

Listing of many videos of the Battle, the monuments, and the area of Verdun
https://www.youtube.com/playlist?list=PLRxPzo3gwAATq_fv1tA mXsJM8N2dhfl0C

Monument to Victory at Verdun
http://upload.wikimedia.org/wikipedia/commons/thumb/9/9f/Ve rdun_4juni2006_043.jpg/300px-Verdun_4juni2006_043.jpg

Monument of the Sons of Verdun
http://i1060.photobucket.com/albums/t456/Lauty10/ARG-U-14_zpsde1d40f4.jpg

Entrance to the Citadel of Verdun
http://www.stripes.com/polopoly_fs/1.273786.1395340027!/image/image.jpg_gen/derivatives/landscape_804/image.jpg

Article on Trench Warfare from Wikipedia
http://en.wikipedia.org/wiki/Trench_warfare

More on Trench Warfare with photos and diagrams
http://io9.com/trench-warfare-in-world-war-i-was-a-smarter-strategy-th-1637657733

Video of WWI Trench Archeological Excavation
https://www.youtube.com/watch?v=y33b_e-cqGM

Pictorial of a Modern Day visit to Verdun
http://ww1.canada.com/after-the-war/images-visiting-the-killing-fields-of-verdun-today

Information about French Gold Coins from the early 1900s
http://taxfreegold.co.uk/france20francsroosters.html

Picture of the ladder similar to the one described in the story inside of Fort du Regret
http://www.jarrelook.co.uk/Urbex/Verdun/Fort%20du%20Regret/Fullsize/04.jpg

About The Author

Eldon DeKay is a former Army Officer who was stationed in Mannheim, Germany. He and his family toured many of the World War I and II battlefields in France and Germany, and it was climbing through the forts at Verdun that inspired this tale. He now resides in Alaska and continues to write a novel every year.

Made in the USA
Middletown, DE
25 April 2022

64716297R10089